Lucky Rescue

By

Trish Collins

Copyright© 2018 by Trish Collins

ISBN-13: 9781974584376

By: Trish Collins

~ ~ ~ ~ ~ ~ ~ ~ ~

Lucky Series

Lucky Day - Book 1

Lucky Charm - Book 2

Lucky Break - Book 3

Lucky Rescue - Book 4

Lucky Shot - Book 5

Lucky Honeymoon - Book 6

Lucky Me - Book 7

Lucky Number - Book 8

Lucky Guy - Book 9 - 2022

Lucky Couple - Book 10 - 2022

Lucky Bet - Book 11 - TBA

Lucky O'Shea's - Book 12 - TBA

Jacobs Series

Riptides of Love

Book 1 - Parts 1 & 2

Love's Dangerous Undercurrents

Book 2 - Parts 1 & 2

Breaking Waves of Love

Book 3 - Parts 1 & 2

Love's Storm Surge

Book 4 - Parts 1 & 2

Impact Zone of Love

Book 5 - Parts 1 & 2

2022

{1}

Grace O'Shea has worked the three to eleven shift at the hospital for weeks now. It worked best with her day classes to finish her nursing degree. She was in the home stretch and couldn't wait to finish. Although she knew she would go on to earn her Master's degree, but she had to take it one step at a time. On top of being Friday, it must have been a full moon because all the crazies were out tonight. When Grace last checked, she had taken a million steps, well, not quite a million, but it sure felt that way. She was ready to go home, and she could leave once she did shift change.

With her eyes closed, Grace rode down the elevator, leaning against the wall. She knew it wouldn't help the extreme fatigue she felt, but that was the best she could do right now. Grace thought once she showered, she could climb into her bed. She didn't have to work at the hospital tomorrow, but she had to work at the pub. Thank God, that would be Saturday night. All she could think about was sleeping in and hopefully recharging her run-down batteries. Finding her car was a chore when she finally walked out of the hospital. Because you couldn't park in a routine place, it was, find a spot and park.

She looked around the lot as she unlocked her car. Once inside, she relocked the doors. Everything in her wanted to put her head back and close her eyes. But this really wasn't the place to do that. Besides getting mugged, someone would come along and call the police, thinking she was drunk or dead. She put her car in gear, telling herself, just get home. Then she could sleep.

It was late. Although a few cars were still on the road, Grace tried to keep her distance from everyone. She pulled onto the freeway and drove a mile. Grace heard a loud crash, metal twisting, smoke filled the air, and suddenly a black car came up, flipping over the cement medium right in front of her car. It continuously rolled time and time again. Grace blinked several times to make sure she really saw what had just happened. Then, she quickly pulled to the side of the road. Grace saw flames coming from the hood of the smashed car and grabbed her phone as she began running. Dialing nine-one-one, she yelled her location as she yanked on the car door.

"Rollover, entrapment, car on fire!" She yelled into her phone before throwing it to the ground so she could jerk on the car door with two hands. She frantically fought to get the smashed door open. Grace could see part of the driver's face inside, his airbag had deployed, and he had blood running from his forehead.

Grace's training kicked in as she stabilized his neck, but the fire was spreading fast. She made the only decision, yanking the man's shoulders from his seat. Grace tugged and heaved, fighting to get him free from the car. The man was semi-conscious, he was mumbling something about seeing an angel, and Grace was worried she would lose him. She dragged him as far away from the burning car as she could. Grace was breathing hard and noticed he was going into shock and knew she would need help soon. His heartbeat was weak. She didn't think he was breathing, so she started CPR.

Grace could hear the sirens from the emergency vehicles in the background. The horns blared from the fire trucks as she knew they were on their way. She meticulously went through the steps of resuscitating this man. She told herself, "Push hard, Grace, one-two-three," she pushed on the middle of his chest with the heel of her one hand with the other one over top. "Deliver rescue breaths," she leaned over him, pinching his nose, tilting his head back. She put her mouth over his. Grace blew two breaths into his mouth and then returned to his chest to perform compressions. "One-two-three," she repeated the breaths and quickly checked for a pulse. "Stay with me, please just stay with me."

Grace kept working when the paramedics arrived. She told them what she did, "His heart rate dropped below fifty BPM. He was semi-conscious when I pulled him from his car." The paramedic took over for her, and the other put in an IV.

"Grace, you did great. We got it from here." Grace stepped back, and that's when she started shaking uncontrollably. She covered her arms as she looked around. She hadn't given any thought to the other cars. But once she stepped away from the man she had just pulled from his car, she noticed emergency vehicles on the other side of the divider tending to the automobiles on the other side. One of the paramedics from her father's firehouse saw her standing there.

"Grace, are you okay? You weren't involved in the accident, were you?" Mike started to check her for injuries. She noticed the blood down the front of her scrubs and her hands.

"No Mike, I'm fine. The accident happened right in front of me." She turned to where she left the paramedics working on the man. Then, as if it was all a blur, she said, "I... is everyone alright over there?" Grace pointed to the twisted metal that was a car on the other side of the road. "I didn't even think about anyone besides the guy that was on my side of the highway." Mike took her arm, leading her toward the ambulance. She said, "He rolled four or five times. All I could think about was getting him out of that burning car without hurting him more." Grace was talking, but it was more to herself.

"Wow, you pulled him out? I heard he wasn't breathing. It was a lucky thing you were in the right place at the right time to rescue him. You saved his life."

3

"I...I don't know," Grace's brows frowned. Mike had her sitting on the back bumper of the bus, putting an oxygen mask over her face. "I don't need that," she suddenly realized what he was doing.

"Just give it a minute Gracie," he stopped her from pulling the mask away. "You're in shock. Breathe." When she began to resist, he said, "I can't have your father finding out that I didn't take care of one of his pride and joy daughters, now can I?"

Grace sat there breathing in the air as she watched them load the guy she worked on into a different ambulance. He appeared to be alive. That was a good thing. The adrenaline was wearing off, and Grace could feel the weariness of the evening setting back in. She leaned her head back and closed her eyes.

So much for going home to take a shower and going to bed. Instead, her mind went to watching the car somersaulting through the air. Then, seeing a man with light brown hair sitting in the seat, with blood everywhere. The scene played in her head as if she was watching a movie. Grace could see herself fighting to get the car open and tugging on the man's suit jacket. When Grace proceeded to resuscitate him, she couldn't see his face. She knew she must have looked at him when she put her mouth over his. But none of his features came to mind, only that he had light-colored hair.

"Grace, are you doing, okay?" Mike was back, and Grace knew she must have taken one of her catnaps.

"What time is it?" She asked when she opened her eyes.

"It's a little after two," he offered her a wet wipe to clean the dried blood from her hands. That's when it hit her. She hadn't been wearing any gloves. The thought of protecting herself hadn't come to mind, and that was one of the first things they taught you in nursing school. Never handle patients without gloves. It was the only way to shield yourself. Grace noticed that Mike took the wipe with a gloved hand. She needed to get out of there and go home.

4

"Thanks, Mike. I'll be sure to tell my dad how you took great care of me." Mike smiled, and Grace turned away. She moved back to her vehicle and remembered her phone. In the chaos, Grace had thrown it to the ground. Once on her way home, all she could think about was getting into her bed. She was even considering not showering, but that was out of the question.

It bothered Grace that no matter how hard she thought, she could not come up with an image of the man she pulled from the car. Was he old? She didn't think so, but did that make him young? He was heavy and big. She knew that much about him. But, why was she even wondering, what did it matter anyway? Her medical training kicked in, and that's what her mind was on, not what the guy looked like. Most likely, he would live and never even know she was there. He wouldn't be wondering what she looked like. When she finally climbed into bed, her body was so exhausted that she fell out right away.

When Grace woke the next morning, she knew something was wrong right away. Her shoulders hurt, and it went all the way down her arms. She was no weakling, but she also didn't do any exercise outside of work. Hauling a body out of a car was more physical activity than she's done in a long time. No rest for the weary because she had things to do, like laundry, if she wanted to wear clean clothes. Hauling her own body out of bed, she started her day. The first thing was coffee, and then she could fully think.

When Grace went out into the kitchen, two of her roommates were talking until she walked in, and the conversation stopped.

"What?" She looked from one and then the other. Maybe she had bedhead or something. She had tossed and turned all night, so she ran her hand over her curly hair to tame it. That didn't appear to be it. She looked down at her body. Nothing out of place there either.

Finally, her roommate, Jan, spoke up. "We were just talking about what happened last night."

Grace went to the coffee maker and got herself a mug. Wiping her eyes as she poured the rich black liquid, taking in its heavenly scent. She took a few sips before turning back to her friends.

"What about last night?" Grace had a good idea what they were talking about, but she learned to ask first. All her roommates were nursing students working in various parts of the hospital. So they could be talking about almost anything.

Jan gave her a duh-huh look as if Grace should know what they were talking about. "The car accident last night." She slightly shook her head and put her hand out to say "and"… Jan worked in the ER, so she might have still been there when they brought in the guy from last night.

"Oh, come on. I heard you pulled that guy out of a burning car. All the paramedics were talking about it and how you saved his life. I didn't get to see the guy because my shift was over, but they said he was big. They called you Wonder Woman and said you must have superpowers or something."

If the pain she felt now had anything to do with superpowers, Grace thought, no thanks.

Jan went on, "The ER was buzzing with what happened. Jimmy was telling me all about it when I walked out with him. Mike was cleaning the back of the ambulance out."

"Do you know anything about the person in the other car?" Grace's mind went to how she didn't even think to check on them last night.

"I don't know, but they had to use the jaws of life on that car. It took them longer to get them out. I was gone by the time they were brought in."

"Man, nothing exciting like that happens to me," Deb said, Grace's other roommate.

"I wish it didn't happen right in front of me either. All I wanted to do was come home, shower, and go to bed. I still can't believe how that car came flying over the medium, flipping over and over across the road. If I had left the hospital a few seconds earlier, his car would have landed right on top of mine."

"Wow, that's a scary thought, but you saved his life last night. Someone wanted you there at the right time to pull that guy out of his burning car."

"The weirdest thing is, I don't remember what he looks like. I mean, I was totally concentrating on keeping him alive. I performed CPR on this guy, putting my mouth over his, and I couldn't even tell you if I saw him on the street today. The other thing I thought about all night was that I didn't have any gloves on. So I had this guy's blood all over me."

Both Jan and Deb's eyes got big. They knew what that meant. Grace would have to go for an HIV test to ensure she didn't contract anything while saving this guy's life. If the test came back positive, Grace would have to report it to the hospital. It was her responsibility to inform them now that she had come in contact with someone's blood. So Grace thought she'd poke around to find out if the man had surgery because they would do an HIV test on him. Not that she could easily find out the results.

Grace couldn't worry about that now. If she had to do it again, she knew she would. Right now, she had things to do before going to work at the pub tonight. She went to her mother's house to do her laundry, and somehow her mother knew what had happened last night. And apparently, everyone knew at the pub too because they were talking about it there. This complete stranger had invaded her entire life. Her only hope was that, in time, things would die down.

The only good thing that came from everyone calling her a hero was her tips. Customers tried to buy her drinks. She would have been soused if she'd drank all the drinks bought for her. So, after a little

7

while, she just pretended to consume them. But, once again, she was exhausted at the end of the night.

Sunday at church, there was more talk about her pulling this man from his burning car. Everyone was making such a big deal out of it as if she had made a conscious decision to save this guy. It happened right in front of her, and she reacted. That was it. Dinner at her parent's house was where her father had pulled her aside.

"I know everyone is making such a fuss about what you did. But I just have to tell you how proud I am of you. I was told the man you saved had to weigh at least twice your weight, and you still pulled him to safety. So then," Cadman put his hand under his second oldest daughter's chin. "You single handedly saved his life. I hope one day he will know what an extraordinary woman you have become, My Grace." He kissed her on the forehead as he said, "I knew you were meant for big things. Your mother and I love you, Gracie."

"Dad, I just did what anyone would do."

"You're wrong there, Grace, because many would just keep going, maybe call nine-one-one."

Having her father's praise was wonderful. He was such a big part of the O'Shea family. Not only was he the fire Chief, but he was the most caring man she knew. His family always came first, and that wasn't easy with such a demanding job. Plus, he was on the hunt for an arsonist running loose in the city. They had pictures of the woman that they thought was setting the fires. When she set the men's bathroom at the pub on fire, she left a note, taunting the fire department for not being able to catch her. They also had her on the pub's video surveillance.

When dinner was on the table, her brother Paul was busting her chops about giving up nursing and becoming a firefighter. After all, she did run in when most ran away. Paul worked with her father and her soon-to-be brother-in-law, Jonathan, at the firehouse. All Grace knew was she wanted this entire thing to go away. Grace was not the attention grabber of the family. She would leave that up to her five brothers.

Monday morning, Grace went into the lab and had blood drawn for her HIV test. She then went to the head of the nursing staff to report the incident. Once Grace had that out of the way and got the results, she could put all this behind her. Grace could go back to her dull, uneventful life, where she worked all the time, and when she wasn't working, she was in class or studying to get ready to take her finals.

She had no time for anything else, no super heroin' for her.

When Robert Newman became conscious, he realized every part of his body hurt. He had been dreaming about the beautiful angel that came to him. The peace she bestowed in him made him want to stay there with her, but he was told to go back. His angel was stunning, her hair of gold, and she had amazing blue eyes, with a warm smile. He knew he'd never forget her face when she looked down on him from over his body. When she kissed him, he thought he was in heaven. Her sweet voice telling him to stay with her, but she drifted away. He opened his eyes to a blurry person leaning over him.

"Robert, honey, Oh God, he's awake! John, Robert's awake!"

Robert heard his mother's voice. She was yelling to his father, and it wasn't helping his aching head.

"Shhh, please," was all Robert could get out of his dry mouth.

"What, Robert?" His mother was still speaking loudly as if he was hard of hearing.

9

"I think he wants you to be quiet, Helen." Rob knew his father took great joy in telling his mother to be quiet.

"Oh, sorry," she said in a whisper tone. "John, go tell them he's awake."

Robert went to move, but he was hooked up to all kinds of machines, and the pain stopped him.

"Do you know where you are?" His mother's face was close to his. He could smell the Charlie perfume she liked to wear. As his sight cleared, he could see her bleached blonde hair that she wore short. The concern was evident in her facial features, and her brows were down, along with her mouth. He had no idea why she was so concerned.

Robert could see he was in a medical facility, but he had no recollection of how or why he was there. All he could remember was his angel, Grace. Yes, she had told him her name, and it fit her, Grace. So he said her name again.

"What? Honey, Grace?" She repeated his word.

"What happened?" He asked in a scratchy voice.

His mother put a straw in his mouth as he sucked up some water, and it was like the best thing he ever had. It hurt going down, but he wanted more, but his mother pulled back too soon.

"You were in a car accident, they had to do emergency surgery, and you almost died on us." The pain he heard in his mother's voice, he knew it had to be bad.

"My car?" He questioned.

"Sorry Honey, she's gone. You rolled her over. You're lucky you didn't get hit by the oncoming vehicles. Fortunately, your car ended up on the shoulder of the other side of the road. But then it caught fire."

His eyes closed, and he tried to recall the last thing he remembered. The only thing he could see was Grace's face, her smile. Her bright eyes. "Robert," his mother became concerned.

"I'm here, Mom. I was just trying to remember…When was the accident?"

"Three days ago, you had some meeting to go to, the last I spoke to you."

He had been in the hospital for three days, "Right, I was on my way home."

The nurse came in, "Welcome back, Mr. Newman. I'm going to check your vital signs. How do you feel?"

"Like a bus ran over me, then backed up and did it again." She laughed as if he was making a joke, but that was how he felt.

"From what I hear, you're lucky to be alive. One of our own was on the scene and pulled you from your car. That was the first time we almost lost you." She put the blood pressure cuff on his arm and put those things in her ears to listen to his heartbeat, so he couldn't ask her more about the person who saved his life.

Next, the doctor came in to check on him. With the confusion, he never did get any more information about the person that saved him. Then he found out about his extensive injuries and how he died on the table during surgery. They revived him—no wonder he had seen an angel. The nurse told him he almost died on the side of the road before coming to the hospital, which made sense because that was where she appeared to him first.

Robert spent a few more days in the hospital before leaving with a set of crutches. He hated having to use them, but at least he was alive. They made him feel like a kid who did something stupid and earned a pair of crutches for six weeks. He knew things could have been worse after seeing pictures of his beloved Porsche, smashed and burned. The insurance company was still sorting it all out. He knew the other person in the accident had fallen asleep at the wheel and had been badly hurt also. The car was something he could replace, not that he wouldn't miss his vehicle. He had worked his ass off to get that car.

{2}

The fanfare of saving that man's life blew over, and Grace found out her HIV test returned negative. Although the hospital reprimanded her for being careless, but commended her for coming forward and reporting the incident. Their advice to her was always to have gloves in her car or on her person. Every night she left the hospital, she drove by the spot where the black car came flying out of nowhere. She could still see the deep grooves in the pavement where the car slid across the road.

Grace knew the man survived and was released from the hospital. She didn't know anything else about him, and she stopped obsessing over not being able to see his face. What did it matter anyway? She had to focus on her finals. That's where all her free time was spent, hitting the books. The idea of no more school for a while was what drove her. She would still work at both places, but no classes —well, not until she went back to school. Grace planned to take a little break. *What doesn't kill you makes you stronger, right?*

Robert was recovering nicely from his accident. It was a good thing because if his mother didn't stop hovering over him. He just might have to kill himself. He tried to tell her he was fine, but he was her only child and her entire world. He had gotten rid of the crutches and had a walking cast on his ankle. The gash over his eye was healing, as the stitches came out over a week ago. He still had to take it easy but went into his office for a few hours every day.

Grace still came to him every night when he slept. He also found himself thinking about her during the day. The more he thought about her, the more real she seemed to be. She didn't float through the air or anything like that. But he still saw the glow of the halo around her head. Although she hadn't said anything new to him, it was a repeat of all the times from before. He didn't tell anyone about seeing Grace for fear they would think he was crazy. Who would believe him anyway? He thought of the only person that wouldn't laugh at him, a priest.

Robert googled Catholic Churches, and there was a long list of them in the city. He decided to call the one closest to him. Robert wasn't sure what he would say, but he had to tell someone about the angel he saw.

"Hello, Our Lady of Mercy Catholic Church. May I help you?" An older lady's voice was on the other end of the phone.

"Hello, yes, I hope someone can help me. I need to speak to a priest."

"We have confession on Wednesday mornings and Saturday evenings. No appointment necessary."

"Oh, I don't need confession. I need to talk to a priest about a near-death experience." He hoped that didn't sound too crazy.

"When would you like to come in? Father O'Shea is here today, and Father Michaels will be in tomorrow. Or you can make an appointment at your convenience. Someone is pretty much here all the time."

"I'd like to come in today if that's okay?" The sooner he spoke to someone, the better he thought he'd feel about seeing Grace.

"That will be fine. Let me pull up his schedule on this darn computer, hang on a minute. I liked it so much better when all I had to do was open an appointment book. They say this is faster, but I don't see how. Okay, here we are. What time would you like to come in? He has…"

"The first available appointment, please," he didn't want to sound overzealous, but now that he decided to do this, he wanted to get it over. Maybe the priest could help him get Grace out of his head. That thought saddened him because he didn't really want Grace to go, but he needed to know if he was crazy.

"You can come now, he is in a meeting, but it should be over by the time you get here, Mr.…." The woman waited for him to give her his name, no doubt to put in the darn computer. Robert laughed at the thought.

"Newman, my name is Robert Newman."

"Okay, Mr. Newman, we will see you soon," the phone line went dead.

Robert got to the church in no time but waited in the parking lot for a few minutes to gather his wits. When he thought he had it all together, he went inside. Opening the big wooden door, Robert went into the church itself. He had no idea where the office was. A few people were sitting, praying, and he didn't want to bother them, so he walked around until he spotted a man with a white collar and knew he was a priest.

"Excuse me, I'm looking for Father O'Shea's office," the man smiled at him.

"You have done one better. You found me." He put out his hand, "Father O'Shea, nice to meet you." Robert shook his hand, and there

15

was something about the man that he couldn't place. He didn't recognize the man from anywhere, but there was still something.

"I'm Robert Newman. Have we met before?" He knew he hadn't, but the man looked so familiar.

"I don't think so, but welcome. Do you want to go somewhere else, or would you like to talk here?" There was no way he wanted anyone to overhear what he was about to tell this priest.

"Can we go somewhere a little more private?" Father O'Shea nodded his head and put out a hand for Robert to go in front of him.

"We can go to the small lounge we have just beyond the alter. My office is not as nice, and this way, we don't need to walk by all the ladies in the outer office. I was told you had a near-death experience."

"Yes, they say I almost died before I got to the hospital, and then once on the operating table, I did die." They sat in old gold upholstered chairs across from each other.

"I see, and you want me to help you understand your experience?"

"No, well, I guess I do. I saw…," Robert let out a shaky breath, "an angel. She spoke to me. I know this is going to sound crazy, but she had a gold halo that glowed. She smiled at me, told me to stay with her, and then made me go. I see her in my dreams. I think about her beautiful face smiling at me and her striking blue-green eyes. They were a lot like yours. She even kissed me, I think."

"She kissed you? Interesting, did you see a bright light as they say?" Father O'Shea seemed extremely fascinated by what he was telling him.

"I didn't see any light like they talk about, just the light in her halo." Robert ran his hand through his hair. "She didn't have wings, or I didn't notice if she did. Please, tell me this is just something I'm experiencing from the shock to my body."

16

"Everyone is different Robert, but you are not crazy. I've heard many stories of people dying and coming back."

"I feel crazy because sometimes I think she was real."

"Do you believe in the afterlife Robert?" Did he? He never gave it that much thought before now.

When he left Father O'Shea, Robert didn't know any more than before, but he didn't feel crazy anymore. They talked about when a person's body is between life and death. Your mind will compensate for the pain it's in, whether that is in the form of a soothing angel or completely shutting down and losing consciousness. If there was someone with him, then he could have made them out to be his angel.

One thing he had to do, was to find out if Grace was just a figment of his imagination or if she was real. He would start his investigation at the hospital. They had to know something about that person that pulled him from his car. Although, the likelihood that it was a woman named Grace was slim. He wasn't a featherweight of a man, and for her to move his dead weight was doubtful.

He pulled into the emergency entrance and talked to the people who worked on him. Hopefully, they could tell him something. He spoke to one of the medical personnel that worked the sign-in desk.

"Hi, my name is Robert Newman. I was brought into the emergency room after a car accident two weeks ago. I'd like to know if I could speak to someone about who brought me in? I know I came in by ambulance."

"Just a minute, I'll go get someone to talk to you." The woman smiled at him and walked through a door. He didn't even know if anyone could help him or even remember him. An older woman came out with the woman he had just talked to.

"Can I help you?"

17

He explained to her what he needed, and she tapped on a computer screen. "I see you were here, and…the paramedics that brought you in…was company Three-Forty-Three. You can talk to Jimmy Olson. Do you know where the firehouse is located?" She wrote down the address on a slip of paper, and then he was off to the firehouse. He was surprised the woman gave him the information he was asking for, although she couldn't answer the question about who was on the scene and pulled him from his car.

A woman was walking out on his way into the firehouse, and he couldn't help staring at her. He thought he was seeing things because she looked like his Grace, but it wasn't her. But the similarities were uncanny. She called him a creep and kept walking until she got into an old beat-up car. That was crazy. Now he was starting to see people that looked like her but weren't.

Robert went inside and asked to speak to Jimmy. He waited there while guys moved around the fire station, and he spotted a man that looked like Grace. At least he had the same striking eyes. This guy was big, and Robert watched him. Someone shouted, "O'Shea," and the guy walked out of what looked to be their kitchen, living room, combo. An older man came from a hallway and took a donut out of the box on the table. When he looked up at him, Robert had to blink a couple of times. The man had Grace's eyes, too. What the hell was going on with him?

"Can I help you?" The older guy asked.

"I need to speak to Jimmy Olson. He was one of the guys who took me to the hospital. I just have a few questions."

"Okay, I hope he gave you a good ride and took care of you. He's one of the best we got." The man took a big bite of his bear claw.

"Oh, I have no problems with the service I received." That's when another guy came into the room.

"I'm Jimmy, hey Chief."

"I'll let you two get to whatever brought you here," the Chief went back the way he came.

Jimmy asked, "What can I do for you?"

"My name is Robert Newman. I was told you and your partner brought me into the hospital after a car accident I was involved in." Jimmy just looked at him as if he was going to need more information. "I flipped my car four or five times up on the freeway." Jimmy still didn't say anything. "It was two weeks ago. I was driving the black Porsche." That's when it seemed to dawn on Jimmy who he was.

"Oh, man, that was a bad accident. Glad to see you up and around." Again, Jimmy stood there waiting to find out what he wanted.

"Do you know who the guy who pulled me out of my car was?"

Jimmy laughed before he answered, "Oh, that would be little Gracie, and just so you know, she is no guy."

"Grace, she's real," Robert said under his breath. "You know who she is and where I can find her? I'd like to thank her for saving my life." Jimmy thought about it for a minute and guessed he wasn't a serial killer.

"Little Gracie O'Shea, you can find her at O'Shea's Irish pub. She works there, but just so you know, she has five brothers, if you're thinking about any funny stuff, they will beat the crap out of you, or Raylan, her sister, will. You don't want her to get a hold of you, for sure."

"O'Shea, I just talked to a priest named O'Shea."

"Yep, that would be her uncle."

"And someone called the name O'Shea a minute ago."

"Yep again, that would have been Paul, one of her brothers and the Chief. You met him, he's, her father."

No wonder he was seeing Grace in everyone, "Hey, there was just a woman here." Robert pointed his thumb over his shoulder, "She was leaving as I came in, was she related to Grace, too?"

Jimmy turned and looked at the table and saw the boxes of donuts, and turned back to him. "Well, damn, you already met Raylan. She keeps us up on the donuts, and if you get a chance to eat at O'Shea's, Raylan is an awesome cook."

For the next week, Robert went into O'Shea's and didn't see Grace. He saw many people that looked like Grace, but not her. When Friday came, Robert didn't have very high hopes of catching a glimpse of the woman that was monopolizing his dreams for three weeks now. He went in much later than he had been going, and the second Robert walked through the door, he knew she was there. Moving down the bar, he saw her. She stood facing the mirrors that lined the back wall of the bar. His heart began to pound in his chest from the anticipation of meeting her.

Robert stood back and watched her move up and down the bar, serving drinks, laughing as she talked to everyone. She had curly light red hair, and now he knew why she looked like she had a halo. The lights from overhead made her hair glow in a golden tone. She didn't seem very big from what he could see of her. She was actually tiny. He wondered how she got him out of the car. Maybe she wasn't alone?"

Robert couldn't wait any longer. He went to the bar to order a drink.

"Hi, what can I get you?"

He stood there because this was his Grace. The voice that he heard telling him to stay with her.

"I'm Robert," that's all he said, but she didn't seem to know who he was.

20

"What can I get you, Robert?"

He managed to get out the words, "A beer," then said, "You're Grace, right?"

"That's me," she put his drink on the bar. "You running a tab or paying now?"

"I'll run a tab," he said as he watched her every move.

"I need your license, Robert."

He liked the way she kept saying his name. But he was a little confused why she hadn't recognized him. "You don't know who I am, do you?" He handed her his driver's license.

She looked down at it and said, "You are Robert Newman, right?"

"Grace, I'm the man you pulled from my car on the highway." He watched as her eyes got big. "I'd like to buy you dinner to thank you for saving my life."

"Um, give me a minute," she walked away and grabbed the other bartender's sleeve, then he saw the brother that was at the firehouse go and join them. Grace was talking, he knew, because her hands were flying around. He knew the moment she mentioned him because they all looked his way. The guy with the beard came back with Grace.

Mack put out his hand to shake with Robert, "Hi, Robert, I'm Mack, Grace's oldest brother. She says you want to buy her dinner. I think that's very nice of you, as you know, Grace is working. But she does need to eat, so what do you think about eating here? Ray has a special on lobster tonight. You won't be disappointed."

"I'd like that, Mack. I understand you don't know me, but Grace saved my life, and I figure dinner is the least I could do to thank her." He could see her standing behind her brother as if she was scared of him. Just as she came around the bar, the music from the other room started to play. It was loud and would hinder them from talking. She picked the table farthest from the opening where the music was playing. He watched Grace grab a menu for him, and when she sat down, he couldn't help staring at her. The memories came flooding back of her over him.

"Grace, I'm sorry for staring at you. I hope you understand when I say I wasn't sure if I imagined you or if you were real."

"I'm sorry, too. I didn't know who you were because when your car came crashing down in front of my vehicle, I went into nurse mode. I wasn't looking at you as much as I was focused on what I was doing."

"I guess that makes sense. I know this will sound crazy, but up until a week ago, I thought you were a beautiful angel."

"I'm no angel," she laughed nervously. "I'm just a nursing student trying to finish school, working at the hospital and here. I was so exhausted. I almost didn't believe what I was seeing."

"Will you tell me what you saw? I mean, how everything happened."

"Like I said, I was on my way home from the hospital. I was exhausted, so I tried to avoid all the other cars when I heard a loud crash and metal twisting. Your car shot up and over the divider. You almost landed on top of my vehicle. Anyway, I watched in horror as your car rolled repeatedly. I pulled over, calling nine-one-one. I couldn't get your door open. I could see through the window that your airbag had deployed. You were bleeding, and the car was on fire. I yanked harder to get the door to open. Once I stabilized your neck, I had to get you out."

"This is the part I really want to know. How did someone of your size get me, not only out of a crunched car but far enough away from a burning vehicle?"

"I'm not really sure, but I yanked and pulled until you were out. You said something about seeing an angel, and then your pulse became undetectable. I performed CPR until the paramedics came and took over."

"Did you say to stay with you?"

"I guess I'm not sure. I was talking myself through the steps of CPR. The night was more of a blur to me."

"CPR, huh? I guess that explains another thing." Well, damn, he had thought she kissed him. Guess not.

"What's that?" Grace had relaxed as they talked to one another.

"Damn, I thought you kissed me, but you were just doing CPR on me." He could hear the disappointment in his own voice.

{3}

"You thought that an angel, I mean that I kissed you?" Grace's words came out loud just as the song in the other room stopped. Her face instantly turned red.

Robert liked the way she blushed and the idea of her lips on his, even if technically it wasn't a kiss. "You have to understand, I was in shock, and a beautiful angel came to me to save my life. It's just a bonus that you weren't a real angel at all, but someone who is sitting across the table from me. Now, I can look at you for real instead of seeing you in my dreams."

"You dreamt about me?" The surprise showed on her face.

"Why do you look so shocked? When I woke up in the hospital, I said your name. I'm glad to know you were actually there at the accident. This way, I don't feel as crazy. Your uncle told me…"

"My uncle?" Grace's words became loud again.

"I didn't know he was your uncle until I went to your father's firehouse."

"The firehouse, my father?" Grace was yelling now.

24

"Yeah, I went there to talk to Jimmy Olson, the paramedic that took me to the hospital. I was trying to find out if you were real or just in my head. I had no idea these people were related to you until Jimmy told me. I thought I was seeing you everywhere, even in guys. I must say, I was happy to find out they were related to you. Although, your sister called me a creep."

Grace frowned, "You spoke to my sister?"

Patrick came to their table to take their order. He was going through the motions when he realized Grace was sitting at the table, "Hi, I'm Patr...Grace, what are you doing?" He looked at the guy she was with, "And who is this?"

"Patrick, meet Robert Newman, Robert, this is my brother. Robert is the man I pulled from the burning car."

"Nice to meet you, Patrick," Robert put out his hand, and at first, Patrick just looked at it.

"Don't be a jerk, Patrick. Robert is buying me dinner to thank me, that's all." Patrick reluctantly shook Robert's hand.

"Fine, what can I get you?"

"What would you recommend, Patrick?" Robert was trying to win Patrick over.

"Well, anything Raylan makes is great, but I would order tonight's special."

"Grace, what would you like to have?" Robert wanted dinner to last, and if that meant ordering everything on the menu, he would.

"I'm not really hungry. I'll have whatever you're having."

"Fine, we'll have two of Raylan's specials, and I'll let you pick us an appetizer. Grace, what would you like to drink?"

Her brother chuckled, putting his order pad over his face when Grace gave him a dirty look. "I'll have my usual drink, and I can't eat all that food."

"Two specials, coming right up," Patrick said and walked away.

"I hope you plan on eating a lot because you just ordered a ton of food."

"If it gives me more time with you, I will eat every bite."

Instead of putting the order through the computer, Patrick went into the kitchen to personally tell Raylan about this guy Robert.

"Ray, do you know about the guy that's buying Grace dinner? He's the guy she pulled from the burning car."

Raylan stopped what she was doing at the grill, "He should be doing more than that. After all, she did save his life. What does he look like?"

"I don't know, but he just ordered two of your specials and told me to pick an appetizer, so I thought he would like the sampler." It was the most expensive appetizer on the menu. Patrick grinned because he knew what he was doing, even if he played naïve.

"Herb," Ray was going to check this guy out, and her helper Herb was the only one she trusted to run her kitchen.

"I got it covered. You go and see who this guy is with our Gracie." Raylan smiled at the older man because he knew her in the short amount of time, he'd been working with her. Most times, that would freak her out, but Herb was great because he could see what she needed before she asked for it.

Ray followed Patrick out into the bar area, where Mack and Paul were standing together watching Grace. Gabe joined them, "What are all you guys looking at?" He asked as he looked in the direction they were staring.

26

"Who's that with Grace?" All of a sudden, Gabe became concerned.

Mack answered, "The guy she pulled from the car."

"That guy was at the firehouse when I brought over donuts last week. He was staring at me. I called him a creep. I'll straighten this out right now." Raylan started to walk in Grace's direction. When Mack grabbed the back of her shirt, he didn't pull rank very often, but he did this time.

"Hold up, Ray. He went to the firehouse looking for answers to who saved him. When he saw you, he probably thought you were Grace?"

"Why, we don't look anything alike?" All her brothers began to laugh at Raylan's statement.

Macy and Bryant came in through the kitchen. They had planned to have Raylan's lobster special for dinner. Herb filled them in on what was happening out in the bar. Tane took off his rubber gloves from doing the dishes and went out with Bryant and Macy into the bar. Ava came up at the same time as the rest of Grace's siblings assembled to watch her.

Robert saw the O'Shea family gathering one by one, "Umm, Grace, I think your family might be plotting a way to get rid of me." Grace whipped her head around to see all of her brothers and sisters watching them. She nudged her head to the left once, and when no one moved, she did it again.

"Excuse me a minute," Grace got up, signaling everyone to move except for Raylan, she stayed put.

"Ray, why are you not in the kitchen? Please don't make this harder than it already is."

"Fine, but if he so much as touches one hair on your head, then all bets are off." Raylan made sure to keep eye contact with Robert just

27

so he knew she wasn't playing. She turned and went back into the kitchen. Grace took a shaky breath and went back to the table.

"I'm sorry about the gawkers. They mean well."

"No, I get it. They're your family, and they love you. There's nothing wrong with that. But I think your sister is scarier than your biggest brother. They know I'm recovering from an almost fatal crash, right?"

Grace laughed, "Raylan will love that you said she's scarier than Paul. But in fact, she can be a tough one, that's for sure."

"Jimmy told me that you had five brothers, and I knew about your one sister, but who were the rest of the people?"

"Well, you met Mack at the bar. Bryant was with his wife, Macy. Then there's Ray, the scary one, and then Paul, who you saw at the firehouse. The twins, Gabe and Patrick. Patrick took our order. You haven't met my sister Ava or my brother Tane."

"Wow, no wonder I was seeing you everywhere. What does that make, nine kids in your family?"

"Yes, and we're multiplying quickly, Julia, who isn't here, is Mack's fiancée, and Johnathan is engaged to the scary one." Grace giggled again and smiled at Robert's expression.

Just then, the appetizer came. It was a big platter full of all the different starters that O'Shea's offered. It was a meal in itself, and many ordered it to share with a group of people. Grace watched Robert, and he didn't seem to be concerned about the amount of food that was just put in front of him.

"Where should I start? What do you like the best?" Robert waited for her to pick first.

"I can honestly say Raylan doesn't make anything that's bad. She is the food here, and you should see how people will pile in here on St. Patrick's Day just to have Raylan's exclusive food for the day.

She makes different appetizers to the main course." Grace wasn't hungry until the food showed up, and she picked up a chicken wing, and Robert did the same. It wasn't long before Patrick was back with their food. He set up a stand to lay the large tray down on as he put the huge platters of food on the table.

"Enjoy," Patrick said as he walked away.

The table was full, between the food that Patrick had just put in front of them and the appetizer from earlier. Grace watched Robert as he looked over at all the food he had ordered. She smiled just a bit because it might take him all night to eat all this. Not that she could sit here with him that long.

Robert put on the little bib, picked up the lobster cracker, and dug in. He looked up to see her watching him, "What? Why are you smiling?"

Grace hadn't realized that she was smiling. It had been a long time since she did anything for fun, and she was having a good time with Robert. Now that she got a good look at him, he was quite cute with his sandy blonde hair. She could see the scar healing over his right eye, making the slightest break in his brow. He had strong facial features, even a little growth on his face gave him a sexy look. It was her turn to stare as her eyes took in his build. He wasn't a small guy. No wonder her arms and shoulders hurt like hell the next day.

"Grace," when Robert said her name, she realized she had been staring way too long to be polite.

"Sorry, I was just trying to figure out how I got your big body out of your car. I mean, I felt it for days afterward, but looking at you now, I think there is no way I could do it again."

Robert smiled at her, and her heart skipped a beat. *Oh, God.* Her words to Raylan came back to her. *"I can't see past getting through school, much less finding a guy and wanting to get married. He would have to be thrown right in front of me for me to notice him."*

29

Robert was literally thrown in front of her, and she noticed him now. Not that he was interested in her in that way.

"Grace, would you consider going out with me again? I mean, on a real date, just you and me?" Grace hesitated long enough that Robert was resending the invitation. "I understand if you don't want…"

"No, it's not that. I don't have any free time right now. As I said, I'm a nursing student, and I pretty much work a full-time job at the hospital, then I'm here on the weekends. Any time after that, I'm studying. I have my boards coming up."

"If you don't mind me asking, why do you work so much? I would guess your family knows how hard you're working on finishing school." He could appreciate someone that worked hard because he did the same to get where he is now.

"I work for many reasons. For one, I have student loans, and working for the hospital looks good on my resume and gives me hands-on experience. Why I work here goes back to reason one. I have bills to pay, and we all work in the pub. I'm not the only one that is going to school and working. Both the twins and Ava are also in college. Tane is still in high school. Two of my other siblings have other full-time jobs besides this one. Paul, as you already know, works at the firehouse. My brother Bryant owns his own construction company. Mack and Raylan are the only ones that don't work somewhere else, but they are the heart of this place."

Robert liked the way Grace freely opened up about her family. When she spoke, he found himself hanging on every word. Grace was a fascinating woman, the way her eyes lit up at the mention of each of her siblings. Her smile was genuine, and when she aimed that smile at him, he felt it deep down in his chest.

"Grace, when do you have time for fun?"

"I will have fun when I finish school, not that I'm completely done because I plan to go on to earn my Master's degree. I just need a little breather. I'm running on empty now."

"I admire your dedication. You seem committed," Grace started to look around, and he knew she was getting ready to leave him. "I know you have to get back to work, but I'd still love to see you again. Maybe we could get together for lunch. You do eat lunch, right?"

"Um, yeah, but it's usually just grabbing a bite between classes." Grace watched Robert pull out a card from his wallet, and then he handed it to her.

"Please call me anytime that we can get together. I don't care when or where. I want to see you again."

Grace stood. She had barely touched her food because they had talked the entire time. When Robert stood also, there was an awkward moment as if Robert was deciding on something.

"Can I give you a hug? After all, you did save my life, and you didn't really eat." When Grace nodded, Robert stepped in close and put his arms around Grace's shoulders, leaving her to hug him around his waist. The feeling hit him hard when Grace was in his arms. The press of her body had him taking a deep intake of air. "Thank you, Grace. You are my angel." He had to let go before he wanted to. He stepped back and watched her walk away. He noticed most of her family members were still watching them, at least the males. Looking at all the food still sitting on the table, he sat back down.

Robert could see the bar from where he sat, and he knew it might be creepy, but he couldn't help watching her as she did her job. Robert went back to eating the food on the table, it was damn good, and this way, he had every right to stay. When Patrick came back to his table, he brought him another beer.

"You like my sister?"

31

Robert was surprised by the question but decided to answer truthfully. "Yes, I do, Patrick. I know you might think I'm crazy, or it could be the near-death experience, but I feel a connection to your sister."

"Grace is very loved in this family, and we take care of our own. If you get what I mean, so don't hurt her." That was all Patrick had to say.

"I have no intentions of hurting Grace," Robert said under his breath.

Grace went back to work but found herself affected by Robert's hug in a big way. It was something she had never felt before. When they touched as Robert handed her his card, she could feel a tingling sensation go through her hand. Then, his big body wrapped around hers, just the heat alone coming off his body. She could smell the scent of his cologne. It made Grace want to stick her nose into the crease of his neck and take him in. She had never had this kind of reaction to a man before. Every time Grace glanced up, her eyes found his. He hadn't paid his bill and left as she thought he might. Nope, he sat there watching her. She didn't know whether to be concerned or excited.

Patrick came up to her, telling her that Robert had paid his tab, and food bill, and he needed his driver's license back. Grace had forgotten about taking Robert's license for the tab at the bar.

"I'll give it to him," Grace wanted to talk to him one last time. She went to where he was waiting by the door.

"Robert, I think you might need this," she reached out with his license in her hand. "I didn't thank you for dinner before, so thank you." He held her hand that had his driver's license in it.

"Grace, you have my number, so the ball is in your court if you want to see me again."

"I..." she leaned in, and he did the same as if they were drawn together. His face was so close, and she could feel her chest pounding.

"You don't know how much I wish that kiss was real, instead of you giving me CPR." He said with a whole lot of desire for it to happen.

Grace didn't know what she thought when she closed the distance and pressed her lips to his. The fact that she was in a crowded bar where she knew most of the people hadn't crossed her mind, only the man who stood so close to her. He didn't deepen the kiss, nor did he pull back. Grace ran her tongue over his lips, and she heard him growl as if he was trying to remain in control. Just as she was about to pull back, his mouth opened to hers. That first touch of their tongues had him pulling her in close to his body.

After a long moment, someone came by them and bumped into the back of Robert, which reminded him where they were. He drew back, just enough to break their connection. They were both breathing fast, and when his eyes opened, he could see Grace was embarrassed. He turned to shield her from everyone in the bar.

"I shouldn't..." Robert put his finger to Grace's lips, and he couldn't help running it over the very same lips that he had just been kissing.

"Don't say you shouldn't have or that it was a mistake. Please don't say that." She just stared up at him with her beautiful blue-green eyes. "Tell me you'll call me and that this isn't the last time I'll see you?"

"I'll call," she heard herself say, and he smiled.

"I will be waiting, my angel, Grace." He stepped away and was gone.

Grace stood there, looking at the door that Robert had just gone out. Then, before she realized what was happening, she was being pulled in the direction of the kitchen. Raylan held Grace's shirt and mumbled so loud that Grace could hear her saying something but couldn't understand her. She knew what was coming. Raylan would ask her, "what the hell was she doing" and Grace didn't know the answer. Raylan stopped yanking her sleeve once they made it through the kitchen doors.

Ray had her hands on her hips and a scary face. The one she used when she was pissed, it was the look you didn't want her to be directing at you.

"Before you ask, I don't know," Grace figured she would be the first one to talk.

"So, if you don't know, should you be in a lip lock with that guy? Not to mention the fact that you just met him. He could be a sicko. He was at the firehouse, staring at me. Grace, please, be careful."

"I know he was at the firehouse, and there is a good reason he was looking at you so weirdly. He talked to the paramedics who brought him to the hospital because he thought I was his angel. He knew what I looked like, and when he saw you, he knew you weren't me, but you had my eyes. He saw Paul and Dad. He even talked to Uncle Joe, `all without knowing they were related to me. He thought he was going crazy." Grace chuckled at the thought.

"You believe him, I mean, you don't find it a little creepy?" Raylan relaxed a bit. She took her hands from her hips and went back to cooking. Although, Grace knew better to think this was over with her sister.

"I don't know what it is about him, Ray. I have a connection to him, after all, I did save his life. I can't explain it any better than that. I think it's crazy, though, that I couldn't remember what he looked like for the life of me. Yet, he was half-dead, and he remembered me. He said I came to him as an angel. At least, he thought I was, and that's why he needed to find out if I was a real person."

"Do you know what he does for a living or anything about him? Now that he knows so much about you?"

Grace pulled his card from her pocket, "He's an attorney."

"Oh, please tell me he is not an ambulance chaser? Grace, I know you're a grown woman, but please, find out more about this guy before you do anything. Promise me, please."

{4}

Robert left the pub happier than he could ever recall. Grace was not only a real person, but she was just as beautiful as he remembered her to be. While sitting at the table, he tried to take in her every move, her facial expressions, and how those beautiful eyes looked at him.

He had to believe that Grace was on the scene of the accident for a reason. Why had he seen her as an angel, he wasn't sure? Although he now knew why he saw a halo over her head. Grace had reddish-blonde curly hair, and when the light hit it just right, it lit up. On the night of the accident, the light from her headlights most likely gave her the halo that made her appear angelic. Either way, she was his angel. Now he hoped like hell she would call him.

Robert hailed a cab, and as he sat in the backseat, he closed his eyes so he could relive that kiss with Grace. The way she came to him, leaning in to kiss him. He wanted to be the aggressor, wrap his fingers in her hair—to hold her to him until he took his fill because that one kiss was just a tease. It left him wanting so much more. There were benefits to not being the one to make the first move. To know she wanted to kiss him was exciting. It didn't hurt his ego, either. He couldn't wait until she called him.

But, she had said she didn't have any free time with her two jobs. He hated to think of her working herself to death. He chuckled at the irony of the statement because he was a workaholic. Although she was taking on a heavy load, all because she was paying for school. He thought of how easily he could pay off her student loans. Hell, he owed her that much. He knew she would still work at the pub, but she wouldn't have to work at the hospital as much if she didn't want to. Then, of course, she would have more time, more time to spend with him. He would have to do some digging to find out who she owed.

Grace went about her week just as she did before Robert came into her life. But, with one difference, she carried his card in her pocket. Oh, and she thought about that one kiss that played in her head on a continuous loop. Grace thought about the heat of his body and how she fit in his arms, not to mention how great he smelled. Grace shook her head, "Okay, you're doing it again. Stop and concentrate, you have your boards coming up, and you know what will happen if you don't pass." Her head went back to the books spread out in front of her. She only had an hour for her dinner before she had to get back on the floor.

Grace reminded herself that she had to make a payment on her student loan once she got home. She was one of the few who were paying their loans as they went. Grace still would have a balance when she was done, but it wouldn't be the entire amount. Grabbing one of the apple slices from the bowl, she put it to her mouth as she read over the procedure to start an IV, Grace knew this, but she still went over it.

The night went by in a flash. It was uneventful, just the way Grace liked it. She drove by the spot where Robert came over the wall and couldn't help looking. She should have called him, it had been five days since he had come into the pub, but she did tell him she didn't have a lot of time. "How much would it take to just talk to him? I'll do it tomorrow," Grace said to herself.

When Grace got home and showered, she sat down at her computer to pay her loan. She logged into her account, but it wouldn't accept her payment when she went to make it. Grace clicked on the little question mark next to the box she was trying to put in the amount she paid every month. She couldn't believe what she was reading, "PAID IN FULL." "How is that possible? This must be some kind of mistake." But how nice that would be to be paid in full. With her luck, the clerical error would come back and bite her in the butt. It was too late to call them now. She'd have to wait until morning, which would be another phone call she'd have to make because she said she would call Robert.

The next morning, Grace got ready to head to class when she remembered she needed to call to find out what was up with her student loan. Dialing the number, she wrote down last night from the website, she waited as the automated system went through all her options. Pushing the number that she needed, she waited again. As she listened, the weird voice said, "To better serve you, please have your account number ready." "If you wanted to serve me better, you would have an actual person to speak to…"

"Hello, this is Judy. How may I help you?"

The foreign accent Grace heard didn't sound like her name would be Judy. She sounded as if it should be Mulan or something like that. "Hi, I need to find out why my loan is saying paid in full when I know it's not."

"Can I have your name, account number, and the last four of your social?" You could tell the woman was trying to speak clearly.

Grace gave her the information and listened to the woman type on her computer. She figured that someone had put the wrong account

38

number in when they paid their loan off. What a rude awakening they'd get when they find it's not paid, but hers was.

"Ma'am, it says here your loan is paid. You have a zero balance."

"Yes, I know that, but I know it's not paid because I didn't pay it in full. I still owe a lot of money, so you need to check it again!"

"Maybe your parents paid your loan for you, as a surprise. The balance was paid two days ago by way of a wire transfer."

"I know it wasn't my parents. Someone must have put the wrong account number in and paid mine by mistake."

"I doubt…"

Grace cut the woman off, "Check again because if this is a mistake, I don't want to get penalized for my payment being late when you do find the error."

"Ma'am, all I can see is a payment was made. Why not just accept that someone paid it for you? You owe them a big thank you."

"I need to know who paid my loan. Can you tell me who sent the wire transfer?"

"Let me see… yes, here it is, Robert Newman." They both said his last name together. "So, you do know him, well now you can thank him. He must be a very nice person, make sure you pay him back with a big kiss or something. Is there anything else I can help you with today?"

"No, thank you, bye," Grace disconnected and just sat there. *Why in the hell did Robert do that? Now I owe him.* Grace didn't like the sound of that, and instead of grabbing her books, she went out the door steaming mad. She had his business card in her purse, and she started to call him but decided she needed to do this face to face. She knew she sounded irrational and ungrateful, but she didn't want to owe him anything, especially money. *What would he want in return?*

The phone rang, and Robert picked it up, "Yes, Mary?"

"You have someone here to see you. She won't tell me the reason why she's here, but her name is Grace O'Shea."

Robert's grin was so wide. What a pleasant surprise, "Send her in, Mary, thank you." Before Robert could get up from his chair, Grace came flying through the door.

"Why in the hell would you pay my loan? How did you even get my information? If you think I owe you, you have another thing coming. I can't even begin to tell you how wrong this is. I will not allow you to have any kind of hold over me, you understand?" She was now yelling at him.

He could see Grace was mad, and he had no idea why, but her hair, the beautiful golden halo before, now it to be appeared to be on fire. He got up, and carefully came around his desk, making sure not to fall with the cast still on his ankle. "Grace, calm down. What has you upset?"

"What has me upset?" She yelled at him. "This is not upset, this is downright mad. How dare you pay off my student loans? I don't have all the money, but I brought what I have." She slapped the envelope on his desk, "I will pay you back just as I paid the loan. You had no right. I don't want to owe you for anything." She barely took a breath before she started again, "Why would you do that? What do you think you're going to gain?" Robert stepped toward her, and she stepped back because she didn't want him to touch her, or she might kill him.

"Grace, come sit," he could see she didn't want him anywhere near her, so he sat in the single chair in the seating area. "I certainly didn't do it to make you mad. Look, I saw you working yourself to death, and I think you might have it backward. It is I, that owes you."

"Robert, you do not owe me anything," she said each word slowly as if he'd understand them better. "You bought me dinner to thank me, now this?" She put out her arms as if she was confused and got up. She couldn't sit still. Walking away from him, she said, "I don't want to owe you money, where you might think you can get..."

"Stop!" his stern voice startled her, but he had to clear this up right now. "I do not want anything from you, Grace, and I would never expect something in return. It was a gift..."

"I don't want your gift, I know that sounds ungrateful, but that's the truth. I pay my own way. I don't expect anyone to pay for things, and I'm sure not letting you. I will mail you a check to this address each month."

"Grace, that won't be necessary." She started for the door, and he had to stop her, "Grace, wait," he got up and moved as quickly as his broken ankle would allow. Grace watched, and that's when she noticed the cast. He did his best to hide it, even putting a dark sock over it so it would blend in.

"You have a walking cast? How did I not see that the other night?" She asked as if to herself.

"I didn't want you to see it. Please listen to me," Robert put his hands on her shoulders. "I didn't do it to get anything in return, except for maybe to get some time to spend with you. You have school and then work every day. I just wanted to make things a little easier on you." He could feel how thin she was, and now that she wasn't yelling at him, he noticed her tiny build. The other night at the pub, she had on a long apron covering her front. Today, she was wearing a pair of skinny jeans and a blouse. For the life of him, he couldn't figure out how she ever got him out of the car.

"A little," her eyes got big, "Robert, you just paid off thousands of dollars. You already bought me a huge dinner."

"That you didn't eat, I might add." He liked being this close to her and seeing her beautiful blue-green eyes light up. "You saved my life, Grace, and for that, there is no price tag."

41

"I only did what anyone else would do. I saw your car tumble, catch on fire, and I reacted. I'm a nurse. That's what we do. We take care of people." She felt Robert's hands on her shoulders, he was gently squeezing her in a massaging way, and it felt so good.

"Grace, I don't want you to pay me back. I didn't want you to have to work every night. I'd like to think you could have a little fun, or use the time to study. I'd like to see you eat more. I still can't see how you," he ran his hands down her arms. "How did you get me out of my Porsche?" His hands moved down to her hands and held them.

"I...I don't know, but I felt it the next morning." When he stepped closer, Grace held her breath, and his phone went off. She watched him close his eyes as if he debated whether to answer it. "I have to go anyway. I've already blown off one class this morning." She stepped back, and as she went through the door, she stopped and turned back, "You will get a check from me." He couldn't argue because he had already picked up his phone.

As Robert talked on the phone, he saw the envelope Grace had left on his desk. He hated that she thought he'd want something from her. Well, he did, but not in the way she was thinking. He wanted to take her out on dates, get to know her, maybe even kiss her some more.

"Robert, you with me?" The voice on the other end reminded him he was on a business call. "I just had to sign some papers. I'm listening." He picked up the envelope and slipped it open. Taking a deep breath when he saw his card was the first thing that came out. He flipped it over to where he had put his personal number, and she wrote, "Thanks, but no thanks," on it. Next, he counted the money. There were twenty, one-hundred-dollar bills. He put it all back in the envelope and slipped it into his suit jacket because he'd find a way to give it back to her.

Grace still wasn't happy about Robert paying off her loan, but she did feel better about his intentions. He said he didn't want anything from her in return. She hoped that was true and not just something he was saying because of how angry she was. Robert did seem to get short with her when she hinted, he'd want something from her for the money he gave as a gift. "Who does that?" She said aloud, and the person sitting next to her on the subway looked over at her. "I'm just talking to myself, so you don't have to answer," the guy looked away.

Now, she wasn't sure how she would eat for the rest of the month because she had just about wiped out her account. As much as it felt good to show Robert she didn't need or want his help, she would find herself at the pub a lot in the near future. At least she could eat there for free.

Grace went off to school, and later when she went to the hospital, she planned to cut back one night. She might even speak to Mack about working only one night at the pub. Some time to herself did sound good, and Grace couldn't remember the last time she had fun. Well, she did have that one girl's night with her sisters, Macy and Julia, but she was exhausted. Besides, that was the night of the fire in the pub. They all ended up moving to Mack's apartment. With all the excitement of the fire, Julia had gotten knocked out of her wheelchair, hurting her knee. Grace enjoyed the gathering, but the fire, she could have done without.

Once Grace made it to work, she forgot all about being mad at Robert. She was only thinking about how good he smelled. How his eyes watched her, and how close he came to kissing her again. If his phone hadn't rung, she wasn't sure what would have happened. Even though she was mad, she didn't think she could resist if he moved to press his lips to hers.

"Grace O'Shea," said a man with a big bouquet of flowers half hiding his face.

Grace looked up from the chart that she was filling out, "I'm Grace O'Shea."

The man put the flowers on the top of the nurse's station, turned, and walked away. Grace was still in a bit of a daze. She just stood staring at them. Who would send her flowers? No one sent her flowers.

Betsy, one of the older nurses, came by and asked, "Who got flowers?" She took in their aroma, "Wow, they smell great. You know what that means, right? They aren't hot house-grown flowers. They're more expensive."

"The flowers are for me, but I can't think who would send me flowers."

"Grace, you are a smart girl. Why don't you read the card," the woman pointed to a small white envelope tucked in the center of the bouquet.

"Right," she plucked it from its holder and slid her finger under the small flap. But before she pulled out the card, she looked up to see Betsy still standing there. The older woman smiled and walked away.

The words on the card were handwritten and said, "I'm sorry," she turned it over because there was no signature. Only to find the white card wasn't a gift card at all, but a business card that belonged to one Robert Newman. She found herself mad all over again because as she looked the flowers over, there was another white envelope stuck deeper into the stems of the flowers. She pulled it out and looked inside to see the money she left on his desk this morning. Alongside the money was the other card she had left her little message for him. Under where she wrote, "Thanks, but no thanks," were his words, "Thanks, but I don't need it."

She found herself picking up the phone, listening to it ring, and then his voice mail picked up. Her message to him was more of what she gave him this morning, and then she hung up. She didn't even leave her name, but that might have been a good thing, just in case his secretary listened to his messages before he did.

Robert's phone went off, but he was in the shower. He turned off the water, "Siri, please playback my missed messages on speaker."

"Playing missed message," his phone on the counter said.

"Robert, once again, you managed to piss me off. I gave you that money because I don't want to owe you anything. Tomorrow, I will be going to the bank to take out a loan to pay you back in full. You will take this money because I can't see someone that I owe money to. Don't you get it? I pay my own way! Oh, and by the way, the flowers are beautiful."

Grace's voice ended, and Robert took a deep breath as he leaned against the shower wall, "End of call. What would you like to do now, Robert?"

"Siri, save the number to my contacts, under the name Grace O'Shea – work, please."

"Saving contact for Grace O'Shea."

{5}

Grace didn't get a chance to go to the bank the next day. She was hoping to get a loan to pay Robert back, but she had several big tests. She still had the envelope with the cash in it. On her way to the hospital, she bought a courier packet, putting the original envelope in, and on the card, she wrote, "This would be yours." She made a little heart after the word yours. Putting his name on the front, along with the word personal, she sealed it and would drop it off at his office. This was a great way to give him back the envelope, just as long as she didn't get caught.

Once Grace had cleared his building and started breathing again, she found it exhilarating to pull one over on Robert. The flowers yesterday were a smart way to pass the money back to her. She didn't even notice it at first. She wasn't going to just stand back and let him manipulate her. Grace moved through the city with a smile on her face. She would pay him back every penny she owed him.

Mary, Robert's secretary, showed up in Robert's doorway, "This just came for you, it says personal, so I didn't open it."

"Thanks, Mary," he took the courier package and noticed it didn't have a return address. It wasn't heavy, as if to have court documents in it. His curiosity got the best of him, and when he slid the contents out on his desk, he started to laugh.

"Grace, what am I going to do with you?" He said aloud, not even bothering with the money. He was more interested in what she wrote on his business card. He read it aloud, "This would be yours." Smiling at the small heart she put on the card, it was very telling. His business card had no more room for him to write his message to her. So, he took a piece of his official letterhead stationery and started to write. His handwriting sucked, but he did his best to make it legible and then stapled his card to the bottom.

He then folded it and put it all back into the courier envelope. Next, Robert called his investigator. He needed Grace's address because he didn't want her money or to be fighting with her. He'd much rather be kissing Grace.

Robert's phone chimed, and Grace's address appeared on his screen. He added her name under his own and her address, and then he called the courier service.

Grace went home after her shift at the hospital, feeling tired but a little happy about cutting back on her work schedule. She talked to the head nurse on her floor and was now off on Wednesdays. The idea that she could have a day off in the middle of the week sounded so good. Although she knew she still needed to pay Robert back, he now had the envelope with the cash in it. She would watch and make sure he couldn't return it to her. When she unlocked her door, she found a note on the fridge.

"Grace, a package came for you. I signed for it. It's on your bed, Deb." Grace stood there a second, and it hit her. She moved down the hall to her room. *How would he know where to send it?* "No freaking way, it can't be," she said to herself. When she opened the door to her room, sitting in the middle of her bed was the same courier wrapper she had left at his building earlier. "No freaking way," she whispered to herself as she picked it up, turning it over.

Grace debated whether to open it. Something inside her wanted to see what he wrote to her. She took a deep breath and slid the flap free. She pushed the sides together so she could see down into the manila package. The small bank envelope was there, but there was a folded paper sitting on top. She plucked the letter out and dropped the rest on the bed. Sitting on the edge, she unfolded the thick white stationary. It had his name at the top and some fancy design, stating he was an Attorney at Law, with his law firm and address. Robert had attached his business card to the bottom of the page, and the letter was handwritten. He started by writing:

TO my Angel Grace,

I cannot accept this money from you. I know this might not make you happy with me, but I must do it just the same. Please understand that I wanted to do something for you, something that would make your life easier. For without you, I would not be here. I know you will underplay what you did, but I will be forever grateful. I do not want you to pay me back, not a dime, although I have enjoyed this game. You surprised me Grace, I never expected to get that envelope back, but you have shown me how creative you can be.

I do not want to fight with you over this. It was a gift with no strings attached. If you choose not to see me again, I will respect your decision. It would be a lie if I said I wouldn't be disappointed. I find you to be a fascinating woman, and I have the utmost respect for you. With that said, I will wait to hear from you.

Yours truly,

Robert Newman

Grace read and reread Robert's letter, and she didn't know what to do with it. Everything in her wanted to pay him back, but his words said everything she wanted to hear. He said there were no strings attached, but who does that? Until she decided what to do about Robert, she wouldn't do anything. Although she felt the strong pull to text him. Just to let him know he hadn't won. She looked at the clock, and it was late. Robert most likely wouldn't read it until morning. That was what made the decision for her. She pulled out her phone.

Grace: Robert, I can't let you pay my loans off, even if you say there are no strings attached. I don't feel right about letting you do something this extreme. Please let me pay you back. If I agree to take one day off at the hospital and one day from the pub to make my life easier, you must let me pay you back. That would be a compromise.

Grace hit send and went for the shower. Robert would read it in the morning, and she would feel better.

Robert heard his phone chime on his nightstand where he had it charging. Knowing he should ignore it, he turned on the light and looked to see who had texted him. Robert didn't recognize the number, but he could read the first few words of the text, and right away, he knew it was from Grace. With a big smile on his face, he opened the text. He liked the part about her taking some time off from work, but he still didn't want to take her money. His finger tapped on the screen. What to write back? If he let her think she was paying him back, she would feel better, and her taking time off from work meant he would have a chance to take her out. It felt like a win, win, but it wasn't being honest.

Now, Grace never said what he had to do with the money once she paid him back. He could donate it to a charity or to the hospital in her name. Once the money was in his hands, he could do what he wanted with it.

Robert: I accept your compromise, Grace, but I have a few of my own stipulations. Good night, sweet dreams, my angel.

Robert added Grace's cell phone number to her contact, along with her address. He hit save and turned out the light. Once his eyes adjusted to the darkness, he could see Grace's face and the light in her hair as she leaned over him. The night she saved his life played in his head. He hoped like hell taking the money from her would end the fighting, and they could get back to kissing. That was the next thing he thought about, that one kiss he had with her. The sensation that went through his body and the need to feel it again was strong. He didn't make it a habit of kissing a complete stranger, but somehow, Grace didn't feel unfamiliar to him. It was odd how comfortable she felt in his arms. He fell asleep to her words, "Stay with me, please just stay with me," as her mouth closed over his.

Grace came into her bedroom to get dressed for bed and noticed her phone blinking. She shook her head because she should have known better. Robert read her text. But what was nagging at her was what did he write back? No, she wasn't going to play this game because it didn't matter. He would get his money back, and that was all there was to it. She left the room and went into the kitchen to get something to eat, purposely leaving her phone behind.

Grace scrambled two eggs and popped a few slices of bread in the toaster. As she moved the eggs around in the pan, her mind wandered back to Robert. His text most likely was him refusing to take her money once again, and she would just have to keep trying. She didn't ask, or want, him to pay her loans, so he would just have to take it back, whether he wanted to or not. It didn't matter that he had the money to just pay off her debt. He worked to get where he was, just like she was doing.

When her eggs were done, she buttered the toast and made herself an egg sandwich. Pouring a glass of milk, she sat at the bar, opening her books that she left sitting there. She didn't have a lot of time, but she could study while she ate.

Grace read the same line three times and still didn't know what it said. She put her head down on her arm to rest her eyes, and before she knew it, Michelle, her roommate, was shaking her awake.

"Grace, tell me you didn't fall asleep out here studying again. Girl, you need to get some real sleep. I don't know how you do it. What time did you get in last night?"

"Late," Grace said as she stretched her back and shook her hand because it had fallen asleep from her resting on it.

"You know, if you sleep out here anymore, we might as well rent out your room," Deb said as she went into the kitchen to make the coffee.

"I just need some coffee, and I'll be good," Grace yawned.

"You know we worry about you," Jan added.

"Guys, I'm fine. I'm taking one night off from the hospital. I'll only be working four days instead of five. I promise I will sleep in my own bed tonight, so no renting out my room."

51

"Grace, we know you. You'll just pick up another day at the pub." Deb put a large mug of coffee in front of Grace.

"Nope, because I'm cutting back there, too, I can't keep going like this." She watched as her roommates all looked at each other.

"We'll believe that when we see it."

"You're the only person I know that pays their student loans off before you graduate."

Grace didn't say anything to that because her loan was already paid off. She didn't want to tell her roommates about Robert and his gift. *Robert!* Grace forgot all about him texting her last night. With the excuse that she had to get ready, she went to her room. Her phone sat on her bed right where she left it. She sat on the edge of her bed and opened Robert's text.

"Stipulations? What the hell does that mean?" What was Robert going to want from her? All she wanted to do was finish nursing school, pass her boards, and start her real job. She didn't think seeing a burning car careening over the divider would change her life. This man was impossible. It figured he would have stipulations, he was a lawyer, after all. Well, it didn't matter what he wanted, as long as he didn't want something she wasn't willing to give. Grace didn't have time for this now. She needed to get ready for school. Putting Robert out of her mind, she went about her day.

A few days went by with no word from Grace, and Robert wasn't sure what that meant. Was she just not going to contact him again? He didn't think Grace would let the matter of the money go. Did she need time to think about what his stipulations would be? He hoped like hell she didn't think he wanted something creepy from her. Well, he would have to find her and straighten it out.

He had drawn up a contract laying out how he wanted her to pay him back. He set up a separate bank account for her to make payments. The wording in the contract was in place so Grace wouldn't understand it, but that was for her benefit. He didn't want her to know he would match every penny she put into the account or that he wasn't charging her interest. She wouldn't go for it if she knew what he was doing.

Grace had said she was taking one day off from the hospital, but he had no idea what day that was. He decided to go to the pub every night until he found her there. If he didn't see her, he might be able to find out something from one of her family members.

Robert went home to change out of his suit, and he put on a pair of jeans and a white button-down shirt. He wasn't going to bring the paperwork with him. He wanted to get Grace to meet with him outside the pub to go over the contract but wanted to let her know his intentions.

Walking into the pub, Robert noticed it was crowded for a Wednesday night. He didn't think there would be this many people here in the middle of the week. Robert went to the bar, and he watched people as they moved into the back room. Patrick was behind the bar. At least, he thought it was Patrick.

"What can I get you?" When Robert didn't see any recognition on the guy's face behind the bar, he figured it was Patrick's twin.

"Patrick, right?" Robert knew he wasn't Patrick, but he couldn't remember his twin's name.

"Nope, I'm Gabe."

"Right, Grace said you were twins. Is she here tonight?" He looked around.

"Who's asking?" Gabe didn't seem to want to cooperate with his questions.

"I'm Robert, the guy Grace pulled from…"

"What do you want with Grace? She saved your life. You might want to leave it at that because we would hate to have what she did for you to be in vain."

Robert laughed, but Gabe just stared at him as if he meant every word. "I don't want to do her any harm, I promise. I just want to talk to her." Just then, Patrick came out of the kitchen and saw Robert.

"She's in the backroom," was all he said to Robert. When Gabe gave Patrick a dirty look, he said, "What? He's cool," Robert appreciated his endorsement. "I already told him we take care of our own, and Grace kissed him," Patrick said it, as if Grace kissing him meant she liked Robert.

Robert took his beer and moved into the back room where karaoke was taking place. He stood in the back because he didn't want Grace to know he was there just yet. She was sitting with her scary sister and three other women. One looked to be Grace's younger sister, and he didn't know the names of the other two names. He did remember seeing the one the night he came in to have dinner with Grace. He was sure they were family in some way.

A young girl came around asking if anyone wanted to get up and sing. For five bucks, you could pick a song. Robert took a slip of paper and a pencil from her as he handed it back with his money. She looked at his song and then back at him and shrugged her shoulders.

He patiently waited his turn. It was kind of funny to see people get up and sing songs no one should be singing, like anything from Journey, because no one could hit the high notes like Steve Perry. As time passed, Robert wondered how Grace would react to his song, but it was too late to take it back. When they announced his name and the song he was going to sing, the room became quiet. Grace turned, looking around the room, and he walked to the small stage.

The music started, and he felt a little nervous, closing his eyes. The words came as his deep voice filled the room. He was changing the words as he went along.

"Amazing Grace, how sweet the sound, that saved a man like me, I once was lost, but now I'm found, was blind, but now I see." He opened his eyes to see Grace's mouth open in disbelief.

"Twas grace that taught my heart to fear, and grace my heart relieved. How precious did that Grace appear the hour I first believed!" Grace stood and walked to the stage, grabbing his arm and yanking him off and out of the room.

"Easy Grace, my ankle," he still had the cast on his ankle. She eased up but didn't stop moving right through the kitchen doors, past the guy cooking as he looked up at them. Grace pulled him through a doorway and closed the door.

"What the hell are you doing?" Once again, he managed to piss her off.

"I was singing. I paid my five bucks to sing." He moved toward her, and she stepped back.

"Why, Robert? Why that song? You could have picked from hundreds of songs."

"Grace, I didn't do it to make you mad. Look, I came because you never got back to me about the compromise, and I wanted to discuss my stipulations for payment."

"Why didn't you call me? No, instead, you have to show up here, singing to me in that sexy voice. I mean, embarrassing me in front of my family and friends. Besides, what stipulations can you have? I'll pay you back, end of story." There was a knock on the door, and Raylan's voice came from the other side of the door.

"Grace, are you alright?" The handle started to jiggle, and Grace went for it, but Raylan had the door open before Grace could stop her.

"I'm fine, Ray, really."

Robert got the death stare from Grace's sister. He put out his hand, and she just looked at it, "Hi, I'm Robert Newman."

"Ray, I'm fine…

Raylan said, "Fine, I know. Look, whoever you are," she moved toward him, and Grace stepped in between them.

"Ray, I need to talk to Robert, alone." She started walking, making her sister back up.

"Fine, but I will be right outside the door, and don't think I won't call in reinforcements. Not that I will need them." Grace heard Robert's relief when the door closed. But she turned on him.

He held up his hands in a defensive position. "I just wanted to talk to you, and as you can see, here might not be the place to do that. Please can we meet somewhere else to talk about this? I know you won't be happy until you pay me back, which I still don't want you to do. But I don't want to fight with you, Grace."

"What are these stipulations?" She had her hands on her hips.

"That's what I want to talk to you about, but in a nice quiet environment, without everyone wanting to kill me."

"Fine."

{6}

Grace had agreed to meet with him on Sunday afternoon. That's when he hoped they could put the whole money thing behind them. Robert had to get her away from the pub and her sister, that stared daggers at him as he left the bar. What did they think he was going to do to her anyway? Robert was a prominent attorney in the city, after all. If they only knew, he'd much rather be doing other things with Grace, like kissing her again.

Robert would have to wait four days before he would see her once more. He knew he'd have to play it cool when they got together and not push her. Because every time he did something, it only seemed to make her madder. Okay, so singing to her in front of everyone might not have been his smartest moment. He wanted to get her attention, but like usual, it backfired. It seemed like every nice thing he did for her, she didn't like. In his experience, women liked getting flowers with a card, saying they were sorry. He sang to her, and she got mad and paying off her loans made her madder yet.

Most women in his circle liked for a man to take care of them. Not that he was attracted to the helpless type, but Grace was anything but weak. She didn't want his money and made that clear. She didn't even know who he was, much less wanting to attach herself to him. This was all new to him, to have to fight to get a woman's attention. Robert didn't think that was the draw, but the fact that she saved his life, and didn't want anything from him, was. Also, the fact that

Grace was beautiful didn't hurt. Now, if he could just get her to smile at him as she did the first night they met.

In the days ahead, Robert had to put Grace out of his mind, he had a big trial coming up, and his client deserved his best. But when he was lying in bed, she was there in his mind. It was odd how Robert could recall all of Grace's features, and he liked to think of her as his angel. He thought about her grabbing him off the stage and dragging him away. Grace had a lot of strength for her size, he wasn't a little man, but that didn't deter her. Sunday couldn't come soon enough for him.

All during church, Grace was nervous about this meeting with Robert. She didn't know why. He couldn't want anything from her that she wasn't willing to give. But she still changed her clothes three times, and finally, she decided on comfort. Her skinny jeans, flat boots, and the loose-fitting lace top with the cami under it would have to do. It made her look bigger than her size three, but it was all about feeling at ease and less about what he thought about her.

She had agreed to meet Robert at the coffee shop around the corner from the pub. It was a public place, so they wouldn't be alone but away from her family. She knew they meant well, and Ray was just watching out for her as she always did, but she had to handle Robert on her own. Her family didn't know about what he did for her, and she didn't want them to know.

Grace took a calming breath before she opened the door to the Steaming Mug coffee shop. Robert was sitting in the back of the room, looking relaxed, reading the newspaper. Why was she worried about this meeting? He certainly didn't appear to be concerned about meeting with her. He looked up as if he sensed her watching him, he smiled, and her heart started beating faster. She told herself to chill out. This was a business meeting and not a date. They were going to discuss her paying him back, she had to tell herself.

Robert stood when she walked to the table he had been sitting at and stepped up to hug her. A light, friendship kind of hug, and Grace reminded herself that this was a business meeting once again.

"Hey, Grace, you look great. Do you want something to drink?" He said as he pulled away. She lingered just a little too long and stumbled. He steadied her shoulders, looking down at her, "Grace, are you okay?"

"I'm fine. I'll have a black coffee, please." Robert nodded and went to get her drink, and she plopped down in the chair before she fell. What was wrong with her? Whenever she got close to this man, she wanted to breathe him in. He smelled so good. Grace took a deep breath, and she swore she could still smell him. Leaning her chin down to put her face on her shoulder, she inhaled, and sure enough, she could smell his scent on her.

When she looked up, Robert watched her from where he stood in line. Grace pretended to be interested in his Wall Street Journal that he had been reading when she walked in. It was a newspaper she had never really bothered to look at before, but then Grace noticed his phone sitting on the table. When he turned to order her coffee, she accidentally, on purpose, brought his screen to life. Of course, it came up with a security code, and when she looked closer at the screen, a cup of coffee was put in front of her. Grace sat back and knew her face turned red from being caught snooping.

Robert sat down with a stupid grin on his face, and she moved to take the lid off her coffee. It was something to do so she didn't have to look at him.

"So, Grace, how was the rest of your week?" When she glanced up at him, he seemed relaxed as he leaned back in his chair and crossed his arms.

"Fine, I guess. How was your week?" This small talk would drive her crazy, but she didn't want to be rude and ask him what he wanted with her. The way he was watching her every move unnerved her. Grace was afraid to bring her cup to her mouth for fear of spilling coffee down the front of her.

"I have a big trial coming up, so most of the week was in preparation for that."

"What kind of trial?" He picked up his coffee and took a sip before answering her question, and she couldn't help staring as he looked at her over the brim of his cup.

"I'm a defense attorney, Grace. You really don't know who I am, do you?"

"You're Robert Newman, Attorney at Law. You drove a black car before the accident. You work for some fancy law firm, and you had the money to pay off my," Grace's voice became low as she finished her sentence. "Loan, the one I didn't ask you to do. That is the reason why we are here, to rectify that situation."

"I don't want to talk about that here, and once we discuss the terms of repayment, that will be the end of it."

Grace could feel her eyebrows frown, "What do you mean you don't want to discuss it here? That's why I came here, to talk about paying you back, and that's fine if you want it to be the end of all this. I never asked you to do it in the first place."

"Oh Grace, it won't be the end between you and me. It will conclude the discussion about money, though. I drew up a contract, and I want to go over it with you, but here is not the place to have that conversation."

"You drew up a contract, wow. I can't believe this. I should have known better when you said you had stipulations. Only a lawyer would..." she was shocked when Robert grabbed her by the arm, hoisting her to her feet, and had them moving for the door.

60

"Be quiet, Grace, until we get outside," he said in her ear.

Okay, so she might have gotten a little loud, but he drew up a freaking contract after all. What did he expect her to do, just sign the damn thing? Well, he was sadly mistaken because she planned to read every word.

He had her in the alleyway and out of sight of passerbys. His big body had her pressed against the brick wall. He caged her in with his arms over her head. His face was so close to hers as he spoke in a controlled tone.

"I am not trying to make this any harder, Grace. I still don't want you to pay me back. I did not draw up this contract for myself, but I hoped it would make you feel better if there was something in writing. I realize you don't know me, but I'm not a bad guy. I'm not out to screw you." When he realized what he had just said, he tried to rephrase, "I mean, I'm not out to get you." That wasn't any better, and the way she was looking at him had him closing the distance between them. In a whisper, he said, "I want to be kissing you Grace, not fighting," he gave Grace time to tell him no, but she said nothing. His lips closed in on hers, and the sensation shot through his body like a rocket. That same feeling he felt the first time they kissed was back.

He pulled back before he wanted to and said, "Please don't fight me on this." All she said was, "Okay," and he released the air in his lungs. "I want to take you to my place, so we can talk and maybe a little more of this," his mouth covered hers, deepening the kiss this time. When they had to come up for air, Grace appeared to be as dazed as he was. But he took her hand, and she went willingly with him out of the alley. They walked a few blocks before Grace asked where they were going.

"My place, that's where I have all the paperwork."

"I know, but what is your physical address?" He was a little confused, but he told her as he watched her pull out her phone and start texting.

61

"What are you doing?" He pulled her to the side of the sidewalk so she could stop walking.

"I'm texting Mack your address and telling him where I'll be."

He smiled at her openness because she had no problem basically telling him she didn't trust him. But then again, she was a true New Yorker, and she really didn't know who he was. At least she wasn't texting her sister Raylan where she'd be. When Grace was done, they started moving again. It wasn't long before they came to his building, and the doorman greeted him by name.

"Good afternoon, Mr. Newman, Ma'am," he tipped his hat in Grace's direction. "Heads up, Mr. Newman, I saw your mother go into the building about twenty minutes ago."

"Thank you, Charlie," Robert reached into his pocket, pulling out a twenty-dollar bill, and slipped it to the man.

Grace just watched the exchange between the two men. She had no idea why the doorman would inform Robert that his mother was here, but she guessed she'd find out. As they walked up to the bank of elevators, Robert never let go of her hand, but he said, "Don't let anything my mother says offend you, okay?"

"Um, sure," she wondered what his mother would have to say about her that would offend her. After all, this woman didn't even know her. Grace hadn't realized how far up in the building they went until the doors slid open to a foyer and not a hallway.

He leaned in just so she could hear, "No talk of money until my mother is gone."

Grace thought she wouldn't be telling anyone about what Robert did for her, so no problem there. The room they walked into was big, bigger than Grace's entire apartment. A woman was sitting on a gray sectional couch, which once again could seat more people than her place could hold. When she heard the sound of the elevator doors closing, she turned to see them walk into the room, and that's when Robert dropped her hand.

"Mother, to what do I owe the pleasure of a visit?" He walked to her and gave her a hug.

"I called and left several messages that you haven't returned," his mother looked Grace over. "Who is this, Robert?"

Grace stayed back, and Robert went to her, "Mother, I'd like you to meet Grace."

Grace stepped forward to shake his mother's hand, but she still gave Grace the once over. "Mother, be nice. Grace O'Shea is the one that pulled me from my **burning** car and saved my life." Robert put a little emphasis on the burning part.

"Oh," Grace could see the woman's entire demeanor change right before her eyes.

"Grace, this is my mother, Helen Newman."

"Nice to meet you, Mrs. Newman," now his mother did take her hand.

"Grace," after saying her name, his mother looked at Robert. "You said her name when you woke up in the hospital."

"Yes, I thought Grace was a figment of my imagination, actually, an angel."

"How did you know her name," his mother was still holding Grace's hand, and it was making her uncomfortable. Grace slipped her hand free and stepped back. Robert's mother didn't even notice.

"I'm a nursing student, and once I got Robert out of his car, I had to start CPR because Robert's pulse became extremely weak. I was talking myself through the steps, and I guess I said my name as I was doing it."

When Grace spoke, it drew his mother's attention back to her, and once again, she was looking Grace over. "She pulled you out of your car? Alone, without any help?"

"Robert's car flipped right in front of my car. He almost landed on me. The adrenaline that was pumping through me is the only explanation I have about being able to drag him out and away from the burning car."

"Oh my, we are glad you were there, but what are you doing here, now, with my son?" Helen's eyes never left Grace's as if she wanted Grace to answer her question.

"Mother," Robert's tone was of warning. "I asked Grace to come here."

"I would imagine you'd be very generous, Robert."

Grace was beginning to see where this was going, and it was all downhill from here. "I don't want anything from your son, Mrs. Newman. I did what I did because I was there and reacted to the situation, just as I'd do again, although I'd have gloves on, and I wouldn't do mouth to mouth." Her voice was small toward the end, as if she was speaking to herself. "Robert, I have to go. I have studying to do," Grace started backing out of the room.

"No, my mother was just leaving, right mother?" Robert gently took his mother's arm and started her moving, "I will call you later, I promise." He kissed his mother's cheek and walked her to the elevator.

When Robert walked back into the room, he noticed how his mother's assumption affected Grace. She stood with her back to him, looking out the floor-to-ceiling window. He could see how rigid her shoulders were and how she held herself around the waist. The comfortable feelings they shared before were gone. He had to make this right. He moved in behind her, putting his arm over hers.

"She is just looking out for me, as your family looks after you. If I don't allow your sister to scare me off, please, Grace, don't let my mother. As you can see, I have money. Is that going to be a problem for you?"

"Your money is none of my concern. I just think you need to stop giving it away, which brings us back to why I'm here." She turned in his arms, "Before I can even think about anything more with you, I have to pay you back."

"Why can't you see the money means nothing to me, and if I knew, it would have caused all of this?" He paused but added, "I still would have done it, but maybe I should have gone about it differently."

Grace stepped away from him. She couldn't think with his scent floating around in her head. "I want to read this contract you drew up and get this over with, well, the money part." Grace heard him release a deep breath as he went into the other room. She wasn't sure if she should follow him or just wait. It wasn't long before he returned with a stack of papers. What could he have put into this contract that would need so many pages?

"Come and sit with me. I want you to understand that it was to make you feel better about the money when I drew this up. But, the more I get to know you, I see I'm going about this all wrong." He put the documents on the table. "I put so much legal mumbo-jumbo in there to intentionally confuse you because I don't really want you to pay me back. I was completely thrown off by how mad you were when I paid your loans off. I told myself you were working too hard and deserved a break. I could easily make things better for you, and yes, it started out because you saved my life. But, when we had dinner, and I realized you were real, I don't know why, but I felt a connection to you. I realized something else, you are very proud. So, here is what I propose we do, I set up a bank account for you to make payments to. I planned on matching the money you put in."

"Wait, that would mean you paid my loan, and you're matching the money I pay you back. Doesn't that mean you're paying twice?"

"I plan on donating the money, Grace, to any charity you wish. But, in the meantime, I don't want this money to come between us. I don't want to wait to see you, to go on dates with you. This contract basically says you pay what you can afford, without working yourself to death, with no interest. Your one good deed could turn into another. You could help a fellow nursing student pay for school or donate it to the hospital. Either way, I want to see you, Grace."

"I...I don't want people to think."

"Grace, I don't care what anyone thinks about us getting together. You had no idea who I was the night you saved my life. As a matter of fact, you still didn't know who I was when I came into the bar. Until today you didn't know I had money, well not like this anyway."

"Robert, I don't want or need your money."

"Clearly, look at what a fight you've put up because I gave you a gift."

"A gift! Robert, I would not call paying thousands of dollars a gift to someone you didn't know. A nice card thanking me would have been enough for me. I didn't pull my car over and jump into action so I could get something out of it."

"Oh, believe me when I say I know. I had work to backtrack to try and find you. At the time, it was for my own sanity, but once I did find you, I wanted to help you, Grace. You are a very impressive woman. You leave a man with a lot to think about, like, for instance, that kiss in the pub."

"I shouldn't have done that. I didn't even know you. I don't make it a habit to kiss people." Grace felt a little embarrassed about lip-locking with him right there in the doorway of the pub.

66

"Which only makes it better for me. Now, do we have an agreement?" When her beautiful eyes became big looking at him, he had to clarify, "About the money, Grace. I want that out from in between us."

"Oh, I'd have to read the contract. What you do with the money once I pay you back is your business." She stood, "I do really have to go and hit the books." She took the contract from the table.

He also stood, "When will you graduate?"

"I have a few more months, and then I have to take my boards."

He walked her to the elevator, "Can I take you home, Grace?"

"I'm fine," she pushed the call button.

Robert stepped in close, wrapping his arms around her tiny waist. "When can I see you again?" He could feel the heat coming off her body. His mind wanted to pull her back into his apartment, particularly the bedroom.

"I...I don't know," Grace couldn't think with him so close. It was embarrassing how she felt the need to breathe him in. Just as he leaned in to kiss her, the chime of the elevator rang to signal it was there. The doors opened, and neither of them moved. His thumb glided over her bottom lip, and then he pressed his lips to hers. The kiss was gentle, soft even. She stepped back into the elevator as the doors closed.

{7}

Robert stood there for a good minute after the doors had closed, he did have his own work to do, but he wished he could have spent the rest of the day with Grace. When his hands were around her waist, he wanted to pull her into him. Something about this woman made him want to move fast, but something told him he needed to take things slow. She seemed to get flustered when he got nearby. He liked the idea that he might affect her because she sure as hell was affecting him. He was impressed by the fact that she took the contract, even knowing he had intentionally worded it to confuse her. There was no doubt in his mind that Grace would read over every line.

Grace was so sure of herself when it came to matters of the mind, but she didn't appear to be as confident when it came to the physical. Robert wondered if Grace was inexperienced when it came to men. She certainly kissed as if she knew what she was doing. That first lip lock in the pub came to mind, the way she initiated the contact and then deepened it to an explosive level. Robert let out a deep sigh, "Yes, that was one hell of a kiss, one that keeps a man wanting more."

When Robert finally walked away from the elevator doors, he knew getting any work done would be almost impossible. The first thing he needed to take care of was his mother. He would not allow her to put her own spin on things, like insinuating that Grace was at his apartment looking for money when it was quite the opposite. He gave his money to Grace freely, and she refused to take it. There was no time like the present. Robert went to get his phone to make that call.

"Hello Mother, I need to speak to you about Grace."

"Robert, Honey, I..." Robert didn't let her finish her sentence before jumping in.

"Mother, Grace saved my life. She could have just kept driving. I wouldn't be here without her." He wanted to stress that point to his mother.

"Robert, don't say that. I'm thankful for what she did, but..."

"But, it's not just that. She is a wonderful person. Grace is not looking for a handout. As a matter of fact, she won't take anything from me. Mother, she didn't even know who I was, not even after I told her my name. Do you know how refreshing that is? Grace is a very independent woman. She goes to school, works a full-time job at the hospital, and two nights at the Pub her family owns. She is paying her own way through nursing school."

"You like this woman, Robert?"

"Yes, I do, but most of all, I respect her. I understand working hard to accomplish your goals. I could make her life so much easier, but she won't let me." He paused for a moment so his words would sink in.

"Mother, I know you love me, but I won't allow you to make any assumptions or disrespect her in any way. I want to make this very clear. Grace is not like anyone else."

"Robert, don't you think this accident and almost dying might be clouding your judgment? Yes, we appreciate her saving your life, but do you think you should be bringing her to your home? What do you really know about her? She's not exactly our kind of people."

69

"That right there is what I'm talking about, our kind of people as if she is less of a person because she doesn't have a big bank account. Grace has pride. Mother, pride so strong, that she wouldn't allow me to do anything for her because I tried, and she got mad. I mean really mad, refusing to take anything from me."

"Robert, dear, she could be just working that angle, you know, to get you to fall for her. I know you don't want to hear this, but I'm your mother, and it's my job to look out for you."

"Mother, I'm a grown man, and I will not have you interfering where Grace is concerned," he could feel his blood pressure going up because his mother would somehow screw this up for him.

"Fine, Robert, but I can't just stop being your mother."

Grace moved through the city with ease. She used public transportation most of the time but drove her own car when she traveled at night. As Grace sat on the train, she thought how she had no idea that Robert had that kind of big bucks, not that it made a difference to her. She still didn't want any part of his money. Looking down at the contract in her hand, she wondered what he had put in it to confuse her. Not that legal crap was her thing, with all the "The first party, doing something or another for the second party, and therefore and whereas," lingo. He might even refer to her as the borrower and himself as the lender, not that she asked for this. She was just trying to get home after work to take a shower and go to bed.

Grace thought about how Robert's mother didn't look all that impressed with her, the way the woman looked her over. Now she understood why Robert had said not to allow what his mother said to bother her. Grace would have thought once Robert told her who she was, she might be a little more grateful, though. This was not her first run-in with people with money and how they can be. She's seen it in the hospital when they thought she was their private nurse, and at the pub, it was something you dealt with when you worked with the public. Robert didn't act rich, and he seemed very humble the night he came into the pub looking for her. He didn't wear any flashy clothes. She's even seen him in jeans. The day she went charging into his office, he wore a suit, but he's an attorney. She didn't think it looked to be a very expensive suit, but what did she know?

Grace decided to Google Robert. Who was he really? Because he was surprised, she didn't know who he was, and asked her on more than one occasion, "You don't know who I am?" At first, she thought it was because she had rescued him, and he thought she should know what he looked like. Not that she had any idea who he was, much less about his looks.

Grace pulled out her phone, typing Robert Newman into the search, and she hit the little magnifying glass. She waited as the circle spun, pulling up all the information. The first thing that popped up was pictures of some man with a mustache, not her Robert Newman. As she read, he was an actor that was on a daytime soap. She knew his name sounded famous, but she was thinking of Paul Newman. She scrolled down to Robert Newman – Defense Attorney.

As she started reading about him, she said, "Holy Crap!" He had defended some famous people. He did all kinds of pro-bono work and quite a few controversial cases. One clear thing, in each article she read, he won, and that was why everyone wanted him. One by one, she read the entries, and there was even a story about his accident. It didn't mention her by name, but it had said how he flipped his vehicle multiple times before being pulled to safety from his burning Porsche by a fellow driver. They outlined all of Robert's injuries and how he almost died twice. Grace had no idea about how badly he was hurt. She knew she'd almost lost him before the paramedics came and that he had broken an ankle because of the cast he still wore. He was more than lucky to be alive, and she wasn't the only one to save his life.

Grace went on to read about Robert's social status in the community. He attended many fundraisers, social events, and political affairs. Just her luck, there were pictures to go along with the articles, and Robert had one beautiful woman after another on his arm or his hand resting on their hip. "What in the world would he want with me?" She questioned, it had to be he was seeing her as his angel, the one that saved his life. Most likely, he would wake up one morning and realize she wasn't his type, or one of these things would come up, and he would take arm candy rather than her. It was alright because that wasn't her kind of thing anyway. Besides, she didn't have time to do crap like that. Her social calendar was full of textbooks, work, and sleep.

As Grace sat there, she told herself it was best if she squared away this issue with the money, she owed him and stopped thinking about him. Robert would only move on eventually, so why not save herself the heartache? Maybe God just wanted her to be there to save his life, but not for anything else. God might have bigger plans for her, and that thing about a guy getting thrown right in front of her, well, Robert might not be, "the guy." She decided she had read enough and closed Google. Robert would move on. She was sure of it.

Grace's attempts to understand the contract Robert had drawn up were impossible. As he had admitted, he made it, so she didn't know if she was paying him back or he was to pay her. But the one thing that she knew was the amount of her student loan and that Robert had set up a bank account for her to deposit her money. She would make her payment as she did before, except it would be into a different account, and she would no longer pay interest. Grace had texted Robert, telling him she would sign the contract and have it delivered to his office. Then, she put the cash that was going back and forth between them into the account. It made her feel better once she made that first deposit. Now, there was no way Robert could give it back to her.

Initially, she was surprised she didn't hear anything back from Robert, but Grace fell back into her routine as the week went on. She told herself he must be busy or had already moved on, which was fine because he was a distraction she couldn't afford to have. She spent her time working, studying, and reading, something she loved to do but didn't have time to do before. Robert sent her a text, and all it said was that he hadn't forgotten about her. She wasn't sure what that was supposed to mean.

Robert hated that he had no time to see Grace. This trial was taking up every second he had. He thought how happy he'd be when the damn thing was over. There would be others, and he wondered how Grace would take that, but this was how his life was. She was busy, too, at least until she graduated. He knew she had started putting money into the account he set up to pay him back, which still rubbed him the wrong way. He didn't want her to have to work harder just to put money in that account, money he didn't need.

When a week passed, and he hadn't heard anything from Grace, he had to find time to see her. He arranged for some of his associates to meet him at O'Shea's Irish Pub on Saturday night. He knew he couldn't give Grace his undivided attention, but Robert could see her and assure her that he missed her.

When Robert walked into O'Shea's Irish Pub and Grill, he noticed Grace wasn't behind the bar. He got there early just so he could talk to her. He grabbed a table that would allow all his co-workers to sit and one where he could see the entire bar. One of his female associates showed up and sat next to him just as Grace came out of the backroom. Robert spotted her immediately, and his eyes tracked her movements as he spoke to Lindsey. Grace didn't even look his way, and somehow that bothered him. She went to the end of the bar and spoke to her brother, then she turned, waiting on her bar order, and that's when their eyes locked. She quickly turned back to the bar as if she didn't see him.

Robert excused himself from the table and went to where Grace was standing. Just as he reached her, she picked up her tray full of drinks. She said his name as in a greeting and tried to sidestep him.

"Wait, Grace, I need to talk to you." He reached for her arm to stop her, but she managed to slip through his fingers and walked away. "Shit," he knew that wasn't a good sign. He turned back to the bar just in time to see her brother shaking his head to let him know he had screwed up, yeah, like he didn't know that.

When Grace walked away from Robert, her heart was beating so hard. She hadn't heard from him in a week, or it might be longer. She stopped keeping track. Just when she stopped looking for him to show up, she turned to see him with someone else. Not that it was any of her business who the other woman was, but he brought her here of all places. Well, he was free to do whatever he wanted. She had no ties to him, except for the money she owed him.

When Grace had to go back into the main part of the bar to fill her orders, she didn't look in his direction, even if she could see him in her peripheral vision. He wasn't with just one woman, but a group of people. She didn't know how, but she felt his eyes tracking her. She did her best to do her job and not think about him sitting on the other side of the room. Each time she went to the bar, one less person was sitting at Robert's table until the table was empty, and Grace was a little disappointed and relieved at the same time. The pub was still packed, and she had a few more hours until closing time. She had a feeling Robert would try to contact her after what happened earlier. Her plan was just not to respond to his texts. He'd get the picture and move on.

Robert stood back in the corner, watching Grace. He had no intention of leaving without speaking with her. Just as long as the place still had people in it, he'd wait. But she would not just push him aside without a conversation. If Grace broke things off between them, he'd close that account he set up and have the bank send her a check for the money she put into it. He did not want her to pay him back in the first place.

Grace moved around the room, and Robert had to turn his back to her or shift behind someone so she didn't see him. It was childish, but he wanted to watch her without her knowing he was there. Grace was relaxed, and she smiled a lot as she spoke to everyone. She leaned in to hear what people wanted to order, and he watched the guys making sure no one touched her. He had to laugh because he had no right to touch her, either.

As the pub thinned out, it was harder to hide, so Robert took one of the tables in the back. When Grace walked up to him to ask if he wanted anything, he saw the surprise on her face that he was still there.

"Robert, what are you doing?" She had to lean into him to hear him, and he took full advantage as he touched her arm.

"I told you, I need to speak with you. I'm not leaving until I do, Grace. So, when you're done, we'll talk."

"Robert, I think it might be best if we just leave things the way they are. I'm not your kind of girl." Grace had to almost yell over the music.

"What's that supposed to mean?" He stood because he couldn't stay seated.

"Robert," Grace looked around, "I'm working."

He leaned in so he was as close as possible to her, "We need to talk because you will have to explain to me what kind of girl you think you are and what's not for me." He pulled back to look down at her. When she wouldn't look at him, he tilted her chin up. Her beautiful blue-green eyes twinkled, and he couldn't help the soft press of his lips to hers. She stepped back, and Robert saw one of her brothers standing in the doorway with his arms folded over his chest, watching them. It was the brother that worked at the firehouse, the big one.

"Grace, we will talk," but she walked away, leaving him standing there. Grace's brother waved a finger for Robert to go to him. He took a deep breath and moved out of the room to where her brother stood. The big guy walked to the front door, and Robert followed as they went outside.

Paul walked a few steps past the pub opening and turned on Robert. "Whatever you want with my sister, you might want to change your mind. I know she saved your life because that's the kind of person she is, but if you think..."

"Look, I know you love your sister, but my business with Grace is none of yours. I will talk to her or see her until she tells me otherwise." When Paul stepped closer, Grace was there getting in between the two men.

"Paul, go inside," she put her hands on his chest to give him a little shove, and when he didn't move, she said, "Don't make me get, Ray."

Paul looked down at Grace, "I will be right by the door and back atcha Gracie. Next time, I'll be bringing Ray with me, and I can guarantee she'll be on my side."

"Bye, Paul," she stood her ground, and as soon as the door closed, she turned on Robert. "What the hell do you want from me Robert?"

"I want to talk to you about what you said, that you're not my kind of girl. Did my mother get to you because this sounds like her work? Did she feed you with her crap about you not being good enough for me? Grace, I decide what's good for me." When he saw the confusion in her eyes, Robert knew he had just opened a can of worms he wasn't going to be able to close.

"No Robert, your mother hasn't said a word, but you sure did. I have to finish my shift. I think we're done here, I'll pay my loan back, and then we can go our separate ways." She turned to go inside but stopped in her tracks with Robert's next words.

"Grace, if we don't talk, I'm closing that account!"

"You can't do that. We have a contract!" She screamed at him.

"I can, and I will. All I want is a chance to talk with you. Come to my place after you get off from work. Please, Grace, give me this time."

"Fine," she yelled over her shoulder as she went back inside the pub.

Wow, she was one hot firecracker when she was mad, and he managed to make her furious quite often. But he had to get her to talk to him, and he hated to force her. He had to make her see. She was his kind of girl. Grace was pure and sweet. She had a way about her, a deep-seated integrity that he found refreshing. Grace was the kind of person, what you saw was what you got, no games, no hiding things, just straightforward. He knew he would have to defuse her anger before she would listen to him.

Robert walked down the sidewalk as he pulled out his phone and called for his driver to pick him up. He would go home and wait for Grace, but he would have food delivered to his apartment in the meantime. They could sit down over a nice meal and have a quiet conversation about the situation. Somehow, Robert didn't see Grace doing that. He saw her fighting him tooth and nail.

When his driver pulled up, Robert already had food ordered and was on the way. He got in and rested his head on the back of the seat. The idea that Grace was coming to his place, and it would be late, made him think about if she spent the night. How would it be to wake up next to Grace? The thought of her wanting to take a shower in his bathroom was enticing. The image of Grace wet and soapy had him becoming aroused. He closed his eyes, seeing her standing naked in front of him—that sweet body of hers, all there for him to see.

"We're home, Sir," his driver announced. Robert took a labored breath and got out. He didn't wait for the driver to open the door. As an afterthought, he didn't want Grace traveling at such a late hour alone.

Robert leaned his head back inside the car and told the driver, "I need you to go back to O'Shea's Pub, and when Miss Grace O'Shea is done working. I will need you to bring her here. I'll tell her you will be waiting for her. Thank you," he closed the door.

{8}

Grace was finishing up, wiping down tables, and taking empty glasses to the kitchen. Ray got a hold of her and wanted to know what was going on with her and Robert. Paul had gone to Raylan and told her he had words with Robert. When she managed to convince Ray that there was nothing to worry about, her brother Mack pulled her aside to make sure she was okay.

Grace loved her family, but there were times she wished to be an only child. All she wanted to do was get out of the pub. Grace knew going to Robert's place was most likely a big mistake. But she had to straighten this out with him. Her phone buzzed in her pocket earlier but didn't have time to look at it. Once she had her purse, she pulled it out to find a message from Robert. Grace stood there looking at his message in disbelief.

Robert: I have my driver out front waiting for you. He will bring you here. I didn't want you traveling by yourself so late at night.

"He doesn't want me to skip out on him. I could always go out the back door and be gone before his driver knew I was gone."

"Whose driver?" Patrick asked.

Grace looked up to see her brother watching her. Patrick was one of the easy-going brothers, well, him and Tane. "I'm going to

Robert's place, and I don't want to tell anyone. Unless I don't show up at church tomorrow, then Mack has Robert's address."

"Okay then," and Patrick was gone. Now, if all the family was that easy.

Grace went out the front door to see a black car sitting by the curb, and when the driver saw Grace, he jumped out to open the door for her.

"Miss Grace O'Shea," she nodded as he held the door open for her. "Mr. Newman is waiting for you."

Once the door closed, Grace said, "I just bet he is." She closed her eyes because she needed a cat nap. The car went over a bump and jarred her awake. She had no idea where she was. The car was still moving, but it was dark, and then there were bright lights. She was in some kind of parking garage. The car stopped moving, and the driver opened the door for her. She saw Robert standing by the elevator, waiting for her. He had changed out of the clothes he wore earlier, which just reminded her that she was still in her work clothes. The O'Shea Irish Pub and Grill t-shirt and jeans were the Pub's uniform. She was sure she smelled like smoke and all kinds of other things. Well, it didn't matter because she had no plans to get close to him.

When she stepped up to him, he said, "Grace, thanks for coming."

"Like I had a choice," she walked into the elevator, and he followed her inside.

"You always have a choice, Grace." He put a key into the control panel and pushed some buttons, and the elevator started moving. He stood far enough away from her, but he looked at her.

"I don't feel as if I had a choice, Robert. You knew what would make me come here, and you used it." She tilted her head to one side and then the other, and her neck cracked loud enough that he heard it.

"You shouldn't do that. It's not good for you." The elevator stopped, and the doors opened.

"Neither are you, but here I am," she moved first as she heard him laugh. She moved into his living room and turned to face him.

"Grace, would you like something to drink? I have wine...?"

"No, I won't be here that long."

"I ordered dinner for us. Please join me?" Robert moved to a joining room.

Grace let out a frustrated breath, especially when her stomach, the traitor that it was, growled extremely loud. Robert had his back to her, but he said, "I heard that. Please, Grace, sit with me."

"Fine, but we will talk, and then I'm leaving." She added under her breath, "I need a shower and some sleep," practically throwing herself into a chair.

Robert said, "Now, let's start over. What would you like to drink?"

"Water, make it a tall glass of cold water so that I can douse myself with it." She watched him pour her a glass, and he had a glass of wine that he had brought to the table. He uncovered the most delicious-smelling food. It was almost like having her sister's food put in front of you. There was no way she was going to deny that she was hungry.

Robert put some food on her plate and asked, "Grace, why don't you tell me what's got you so mad? And then I want you to explain your statement at the pub about not being my kind of girl."

"Seriously, Robert, you want to know why I'm mad. We have a contract that I signed and agreed to pay you the money I owe you, and you can't just close the account. I have rights."

Robert did his best not to laugh, he just nodded his head as if he agreed with her, and she went on.

"I know the money doesn't mean anything to you, but we have an arrangement. You can't just change it because you don't like that I won't play your game." Grace shoved food into her mouth. Damn, it was good.

"And what game is that, Grace?" He loved that she was calling him out.

"The one where you say, "When can I see you again," as if you really wanted to see me, and then nothing for a week. Then I get one measly text saying, "I haven't forgotten about you." After more than ten days, you show up at my place of business just thinking you can walk in and demand to talk to me. Sorry buddy, but it doesn't work that way. You might be able to do your other bimbo's that way."

Robert put his hand over his mouth, fearing he might laugh and make his little fireball even madder. "Grace, I was working. I'm in the middle of a big trial. I think I told you that. That's why I haven't contacted you." He spoke calmly as he watched her eat.

"Whatever," she heaved more food into her mouth. She was still chewing when she said, "I don't need a man in my life, especially the kind of man that has a different bimbo on his arm every week. I'm not that kind of girl." She put out her hand palm up and slightly bowed her head as she shrugged her shoulder, "So, you see, that's why I say, I'm not your kind of girl. I don't wear ball gowns that go all the way down my back until you can almost see the crack of my butt. I don't have time for that nonsense, nor am I interested in it. You, on the other hand, seem to love that. At least you're smiling in the pictures as your hand is comfortably resting on her ass." Grace shook her head, "It doesn't matter." She dropped the food in her hand and started to get up, and that's when he moved to stop her.

"Grace, listen," he put his hands on her shoulders. "I have to do things for work, and going to these functions is a part of it. I network during those boring things and talk to important people. I always have a beautiful woman on my arm for a reason. She is to draw attention while I do business and keep other women at bay." He could see what he was saying wasn't helping his situation.

"I have to go, I have church in the morning, and my mother frowns upon sleeping during mass." She heard his frustrated breath. That wasn't her problem.

"Grace, I can't change the past. I'm just guessing here, but you must have Googled me, and that's where you saw pictures of me with all those women. But make no mistake, I didn't take any of them home."

"It's none of my business, what you do. If you break our agreement, I will sue you. I know you might think that's funny," Robert was smiling at her, and her heart wanted to kiss him, as her head wanted to punch him.

"I want an amendment to our agreement. I want you to stay with me tonight, Grace, and let me show you how much I've missed you."

Grace laughed, "That crap might work on the other bimbos..."

Robert kissed her, stopping her protest. Grace resisted, only for a moment, before she kissed him back. His hand went around her waist, pulling her into him. She fit like no other had before, and he would do everything in his power to convince Grace O'Shea she couldn't live without him.

When she broke the kiss, he said, "Please stay. We don't have to do anything. I just want to spend some time with you. This is no game for me, Grace." Before she could answer, his mouth was on hers.

She pulled back again, and this time, he let her speak. "I...I can't stay. I have no clothes, and I do need to be in church, or you will have my whole family banging down your door in the morning."

"I'll make a deal with you. You stay with me, and I will have a change of clothes for you in the morning to go to church in."

"Robert, this isn't a good idea. I don't think we...," he kissed away her words.

"Don't think, Grace, feel. What is your heart saying?"

"Oh, I can't do what it's saying. That will get me into trouble."

Robert loved how honest Grace was, and she didn't seem to be able to hide who she was or how she felt. "I will even sweeten the deal. I'll go to church with you."

Grace shook her head and pulled away from him, "You don't know what you're saying. That is not something you want to do, and it's not what I want. If you show up for Mass with me, my mother will want to know when the wedding is. You have no idea what you'd start and what would come after. You would be invited to Sunday dinner and will be expected to show up every week. No, Robert, you can't go to church with me."

He laughed, "You are making that up to scare me." He pulled her back to him.

She was shaking her head, "No, Robert, I'm not. If you think Ray is scary, you should meet my mother. She knows all, sees all. If you show up with me, your life will be an open book. There is nothing you do that she won't know about."

Robert smiled, "Your mother can't be any worse than mine."

"I beg to differ. An Irish mother is better than a C.S.I team. She knows you did it, knows how you did it, and whom you did it with. My mother can hear you hiding the evidence and can smell the lie on your tongue. You have no idea what you're up against. Where do you think we all get it from, the know-it-all kinda thing?"

Robert put his thumb under Grace's chin, making her look up at him, "Are you going to stay with me, Grace?"

"I shouldn't," was all she said.

Robert took that as she didn't say no. He scooped her off her feet and walked her into his bedroom. Placing her on her feet, he said, "I know you want to shower. I put out clean towels, and I'll have something for you to change into when you get out." He kissed her forehead and walked out.

Grace stood there thinking, *what the hell are you doing? You can't stay here.* But somehow, her mouth couldn't form the word no. She walked into his bathroom and was shocked at how big it was. She noticed there was nothing on the double sink or anywhere. He had one of those big tubs with the faucet in the center along with the drain so that you could have two people in the tub at once. She walked to the other side of the room to the walk-in shower. It was huge, with a beautiful motif tile design lining the walls. There was a robe hanging on the shower door, she touched it to see if it was wet from Robert using it, but it wasn't wet at all. She knew she was weird, but she smelled it anyway, and it was clean.

Taking off her clothes, she stepped into the best shower she had ever taken. The water was hot the moment she turned it on, and the water pressure was like a massage beating on her body. Grace never wanted to leave this shower, besides the fact that she had no idea what she was going to do once she did.

The second Robert left the bedroom, he was on his phone. He called his personal shopper and told her what he needed. Robert guessed what size Grace wore but told her to bring anything she had in and around that size. He wanted everything from undergarments to something for her to sleep in and for the morning when she would leave for church.

Robert knew it was asking a lot because of the time, but if it could be done, this woman would do it. She said she had new items in her stock for this exact situation and that she'd bring them right over to his apartment. Robert would just add it to his bill because she also picked out all of his suits. When you were as busy as he was, it was nice not to have to go shopping for a new suit.

Robert paced the living room, waiting and hoping the clothes would arrive before Grace got out of the shower. He didn't want to have to explain that he had a personal shopper, a woman at that, one that was bringing Grace's undergarments. The buzzer rang, and Robert went to the elevator to let the woman in. She had two people helping to bring everything into his apartment, Robert gave each one a hundred-dollar bill, and they were gone.

He quickly found the sleepwear and laid it on the bed for when Grace came out of the shower. Just then, the door to the bathroom opened, and Robert stood stock still. He didn't dare turn around because if she wasn't wrapped in a towel or the robe he put out, he wasn't sure what he'd do.

He said in a shaky voice, "Tell me you're covered."

"I am. What are you doing?" Grace walked to the bed, looking down at what he was putting there. She ran her hand over the silk nightgown. "Nice, but I'm not into wearing other people's clothes, especially underwear."

He smiled because he was going to have to tell her it was all new. "I had my person get this for you. It's all new."

"Your person? Do they have a name, this person you have?"

"Yes, they do, but I don't want to get into that with you. Pick what you'd like to sleep in, and we can go to bed. I also have outfits in the living room for tomorrow."

"I see. You thought of everything. So, since you do think of everything, what happens next?"

"Grace, we both know what I'd like, but this is more about being with you, not anything else."

"Is that so? If I opened this robe and dropped it to the floor, you wouldn't act on it?"

"Hell yes, I'd act on it. Grace, I'm working hard here not to rip that damn thing from your body."

"Are we sleeping in the same bed?" She asked as she played with the collar of the robe.

"Yes," his eyes watched her every move.

"What are you wearing to bed?" The opening became a little wider.

"Grace," he said her name in warning because she was pushing him.

"Yes," her voice had a sultry tone.

He went to her, "Grace, do you want me to take this robe off of you? Because if you don't, you need to stop. I'd like nothing better than to have you naked in my bed, but somehow, I don't think you're ready for that and what it would mean for us." His voice was deep and full of need.

"I...I," Grace couldn't say anything.

"I didn't think so. I'm going in the other room while you get dressed." He stepped back and walked out.

Grace covered her face, she had no idea what she was doing, but when that man was close, she did things, things she would never do, or ever did. What would Robert think if he only knew?

Robert went straight for the other bathroom in the guest room. He had to splash some cold water on his face and maybe take a cold shower. "Holy shit," he said to his reflection. "How in the hell are you going to sleep with her without touching every damn part of her body? You are a freaking idiot. What were you thinking? You are never going to be able to pull this off." He heard Grace in the living room, so he knew she had decided on what to wear. If she picked the silk, he was done for. And just what would he wear to bed? He needed to wear a metal-plated sports cup because just being close to her was going to give him a boner. Much like he was sporting right now. He started this, and now he was going to have to face the music. Robert opened the door and slowly moved through the room until he could see out into the living room. He didn't see her, so he moved into the hallway.

Grace was in the kitchen, putting the food away, she had her back to him, but he could see she didn't go for the silk nightgown. But what she picked wasn't much better. Grace had on a top to one of the pajamas sets and a pair of his boxers. The top didn't cover her ass, and the boxers didn't help either because she had rolled them up. He could see just a hint of her ass cheeks and her lower back when she reached up to get something out of his cabinets. He was in trouble, big time.

"Grace," he said her name, she turned to his voice, and he could see she didn't have anything under her top. He couldn't control his reaction to her, as his body drew close to hers and wrapped her in his arms. He knew she could feel his hard-on because she couldn't miss it. Robert's mouth was on hers, and he picked her up, taking her to his bed, where he wanted her to be, under his body. She tried to protest, something about the food going bad, but he didn't give a damn about the food. His lips wanted hers, and there was no room for talking. When her tongue swirled around his, he couldn't think of anything but being inside of his Grace.

He put her in the middle of his bed and climbed on top of her. He still had all his clothes on, and it was a good thing because he'd be inside her already if he were naked. Their kisses became demanding, and Robert's hands snuck under her shirt. The second he was about to touch her breasts, she pulled back.

"Robert, wait!"

He rested his head on her chest. He could feel her heart beating wildly as he tried to catch his own breath. His hands were still up inside her top, but he held onto her ribcage, just below her round mounds.

"This is happening too fast," she said.

He knew she was right, but his body was screaming, Go!

{9}

Robert knew what he had to do, but he didn't want to hurt Grace's feelings. He had to get away from her, "Grace, I'm going to take a cold shower, and then I need to get a little work done. I'll be in, in a while." He got off the bed and didn't look back. He closed the door behind him so that he wouldn't change his mind.

He stood in the hall, fighting with the decision he'd made. Grace was going to think he had abandoned her, which essentially, he was doing. But, if he stayed, he knew what would happen, so this was for the best for her. He went to shower, and then he'd go to his office, and by the time he climbed into bed. She would be asleep.

Grace felt the tears sting her eyes. They weren't just because she chased Robert off, but because she was mad at herself. It was clear Robert wanted her, and she wanted him, so what was the problem? Why wasn't she ready for a physical relationship? Every time she came close to having sex, she stopped it, and guys got either mad or, like Robert ran and then never called her again.

This was all her own fault because she should have never agreed to stay. Once again, Grace screwed things up. She flipped back the covers, taking off the pajamas and throwing back on her clothes. The door was closed, and Grace opened it as quietly as she could. She had no idea where Robert was, but one thing was for sure, she didn't want to bump into him as she snuck out. Grace crept down the hall and out into the living room. Still no sign of Robert, now all she had to do was get to the elevator without making a sound.

When the doors closed, she started to breathe again. She had no idea how Robert would take her leaving, but she couldn't stay, not after what she did. Once Grace made her way out of the building, she had no idea how she would get home. Her car was still at the pub, and Grace didn't want to use public transportation. She called the only person she could think of that wouldn't give her a hard time about picking her up.

When her brother answered, she said, "Patrick, um, can you pick me up? I need a ride." She gave him the address, and he said he'd be right there, no questions asked. It was that she knew she could rely on. But when she saw Gabe in the car with Patrick, she knew this would be more of an interrogation. Patrick was the passive twin, while Gabe was the more assertive one. They were two sides to the same coin.

Grace climbed into the back seat, and Gabe was the first to speak. "Just tell us he didn't hurt you?"

"No, Gabe, he didn't hurt me," she saw Patrick looking at her in the rearview mirror, and her eyes locked onto his, "I swear, he doesn't even know I left," she declared. "Is that why you brought him with you?" She pointed her thumb in her brother's direction, "as back up? You would have been better off with Raylan. Robert's afraid of her."

Gabe didn't bother to turn to speak to her in the back seat. "Hey, he should be afraid of me if he hurt you. I don't like the guy. That's all I have to say. If you ask me, you saved his life. Now he needs to go back to wherever he came from."

"Good thing no one asked you," Grace rested her head on the back of the seat, closing her eyes. It was late, and she would have to be up in a few hours for church.

"She has you there, Gabe," Patrick snickered.

"Yeah, well, he should watch his ass because if he does anything to hurt you, we'll be finishing the job the car accident started."

Robert was in his office for an hour. He figured that was enough time for Grace to fall asleep. He went down the hall and opened the door as quietly as he could. Moving through the dark room, Robert stood next to the bed. He had no idea which side of the bed she was on. Putting his hand on the mattress on the side he normally slept on, Robert didn't feel her body. He stripped down to his boxers and carefully lifted the covers. Slipping between the sheets, he didn't know if he should disturb her. He couldn't resist touching Grace. His hand slowly moved across the bed.

Robert blinked a few times, thinking if he wanted to wake her. Then he whispered her name, "Grace." She didn't answer him, and he moved his hand over the bed again until he hit the other side, "Grace," he said her name in a normal voice. Still nothing, he leaned over and turned on the light.

The bed was empty.

The only thing that remained was the clothes she had been wearing when he left her. "Fuck, she left." He sprang out of bed. Before he jumped to any conclusion, he'd check the other bedroom.

The apartment was empty.

Well, he'd make sure she couldn't get away the next time he saw her. He actually knew what he was going to do in a few short hours.

The next morning, Robert got dressed and was out the door. He wanted to arrive before Grace did, so she wouldn't see him until he wanted her to. That was part of his plan to surprise her and catch her off guard. It could backfire, knowing Grace, but she snuck out on him, and he knew for sure she wouldn't respond to any kind of contact from him. If Grace thought she could shake him off so easily, she was sadly mistaken.

Robert knew he had made a mess of last night, and he needed a chance to explain his side. He knew if he stayed in bed with Grace, he would have pushed for more, and something told him she wasn't ready for that. His norm was to get to the finish line as fast as you could, but with Grace, he wanted it to last. The first time they came together, it had to be perfect. He wasn't used to a woman like Grace. She had a sense of pureness to her, not that she was naïve, in any sense of the word.

Robert snuck into the back of the church and sat where he could see Grace come in. He watched the door as her family started to arrive. Robert saw each one walk to the front of the church sitting in the first pew. They sat next to a woman that had been in the church when he came in. *So, that's Grace's mother, interesting.*

Mack came with a woman in a wheelchair, and they went to the outside aisle as the woman transferred herself onto the seat. Mack folded her chair, putting it to the side. Next, the scary sister came in with a man, and just as he watched. Raylan turned, looking in his direction. Robert had to duck in his seat so she didn't see him. The twins came bouncing in, and when their mother looked at them, they straightened up. A pregnant woman Robert had seen with Grace the night he sang karaoke moved down the aisle with one of Grace's other brothers. The younger sibling came in, but no Grace. Robert almost got up, but then she came running in just as the mass was about to start and sat next to her mother.

Robert hadn't been to a Catholic service before and didn't know the protocol. He tried his best to stand when he was meant to and sit when everyone else did. Robert realized the songs being sung were

93

on a board to the right of Grace's uncle when a young girl took pity on him and helped him. When it came time for communion, Robert knew better than to move through the line but had no idea what he was expected to do while the people in his row went to the front.

When the service was finally over, Robert felt he got a workout, sit, stand, kneel, and stand again. The young girl next to him smiled as she whispered that it was the end. Otherwise, he wouldn't have known. He thanked the little girl. The people started filing out, and Robert worked his way forward. He walked right up to the front of the church and waited until Grace saw him, to step up to her family. He knew he wouldn't be welcomed with open arms, but he was counting on Grace's mother. If she were anything like his, her manners would not allow her children to beat the ever-living crap out of him, not in church anyway.

"Robert, what are you doing here?" Robert could hear the shock in Grace's voice, which drew her mother's attention, along with the rest of her family.

"Yes, Robert, do tell us," Raylan moved in behind Grace, and the man Raylan was with started pulling her back.

"Hey, what's he doing here," Gabe leaned forward from his place in the pew and hopped over the divider to come up behind him.

Grace's family was closing ranks around him, and thank God, that's when Grace's mother stepped in.

"Robert, is it?" Arlene put up her hand to settle down her family, and she turned her attention back to him. "What is it you want with my daughter?"

"Let me introduce myself, I'm Robert Newman." He reached out to shake Grace's mother's outstretched hand. "Grace saved my life. I'm the man she pulled from the burning car." Arlene heard her family's ruckus behind Robert, and all she had to do was give them a look, and it became quiet.

"I see, so what do you want with Grace?" Robert could see where Grace got her sharp wit from.

"I would like to speak to her, and I know if I tried to contact her, she would not respond."

"I see. Have you ever considered that she may not want to talk to you, Mr. Newman?"

"I know she doesn't, Mrs. O'Shea, because I did something…."

"Robert," he heard Grace's warning from behind him.

Robert kept talking, "I would like to apologize and ask for her forgiveness."

"Well, Mr. Newman, I think Grace should give you a chance to explain." When Arlene heard grumbling from her children, she gave them a raised brow, and they started filing out of the church. "It takes a big man to admit he is wrong and ask for understanding. Please, join us for Sunday dinner. Grace will bring you."

"Thank you, Mrs. O'Shea. I'd love to join your family for dinner." Arlene nodded and walked away.

Grace waited until her mother was out of the church before she moved. Grabbing hold of Robert's jacket, she yanked him out of the main area and into the back corridor. Grace kept walking until she came to the small door. Opening it, she shoved him in and followed. The room she had pushed him into was small and dark, but it was private. The broom closet was where Grace would go when she was a child, and her mother would spend countless hours cleaning the church.

"Why Robert? Why would you do that? You make me so mad, I could… No, I won't say it."

Robert said, "Kill me?" He knew he was playing dirty, but she didn't give him much choice. He had no idea where he was, but the room had a musty smell to it, and the air was cold. Stepping forward, he reached for her. "Grace, I needed to explain my actions last night. First, let me say I was wrong because I never should have left you in my bed alone. I feared if I stayed, things would have gotten out of hand, and I don't think you're ready for that. I've never met someone like you." He heard her laugh, but it was more to hide her insecurities. When he reached for her again, he found she was up against the door. She was as far away from him as she could get and had her arms wrapped around her body, hugging herself. He still pulled her in close.

"I don't mean that in a bad way, Grace. You're different because you have a center, pure, and good, like the angel you are."

Grace laughed again, "I told you before, I'm not an angel."

"Grace, I'm going to ask you a question, and I want you to be honest with me. Have you ever been with a man before, Grace?" Her silence told him what he wanted to know, but then she tried to cover it by protesting.

"Of course, I have," she tried to pull away from him, but the room was too small to truly move around.

"Grace, it's okay if you haven't…."

"I have," she attempted to turn in his arms so she could open the door and escape, but he used his big body to prevent her from leaving.

With his hands on the door over her head, he said in her ear, "My little angel, Grace."

She began to say something, "I'm…," and he softly nuzzled her ear with his lips. "I want to try again, Grace. Give me a chance to show you how I feel about you."

"Robert, what do you want from me?" Her head tilted to the side to give him better access to her neck.

"I want you, Grace. I want all of you." His body pressed to hers, just the smell of her hair and the heat from her body had him hard. His hand came off the door and softly caressed her face so his lips could find hers. He whispered, "Do you have any idea what you do to me?"

In the sultriest voice he ever heard, she purred, "Tell me, tell me what I do to you."

He was a goner, "You send me into overdrive. I knew when you were showing up in my dreams, Grace. When you performed CPR, I had you kissing me. You were touching me, and in my mind, it had nothing to do with you saving my life. But it was when I got to touch you that I knew." His hand shifted over her stomach, and he felt her suck in, which put a gap in her pants. His finger spread wide. He loved that his big hands covered so much of her skin. Robert kissed down her neck as he tenderly told her what she did to him.

"When you're close, I can't help my body's reaction to you. That first night at the pub, not only was I extremely glad to find you were real, but that kiss. You do things..." his words cut out when she moaned.

"What things?" she asked in a whisper.

He took her hand off the wall and held it over his hardness. When she gasped, it was clear she hadn't expected his arousal. He intertwined their fingers as he moved her hand over him, shamefully pressing into it. They heard voices and stood stock-still. He didn't even think they were breathing. Hell, they were in the broom closet of her uncle's church. What the heck was the matter with him? He felt like when he was a teenager, trying to find a place to be alone with his girlfriend so they could touch each other or more. That reminded him that Grace most likely never did that. She was his angel.

"We have to get out of here." She pulled her hand free as if the spell was broken, and she realized what she was doing.

Grace pressed back to get him to move so she could open the door. She turned the handle slowly and cracked the door. Grace looked down the hall one way, then poked her head around the door. She then grabbed Robert and pulled him along with her, shutting the door behind them.

"Act normal, as if we weren't just making out in the cleaning closet," she whispered. Robert took her hand in his as they walked out of the church. Once they were on the steps, she turned to face him. "You can't come to dinner. I know my mother invited you, but you can't go. I can't let you do it because you'll be the sacrificial lamb."

Robert started to laugh, "You think I can't hold my own? You do know I'm a defense attorney, right? I mean, I've taken on a lot of tough people. I can handle your family, Grace. If we are going to be together, they have to get used to having me around."

She looked up at him, "What do you mean together?"

"You know exactly what I mean, Grace. We're dating, going steady, a couple." He watched as she started backing up. He got the feeling she was going to make a run for it, so he took her arm and pulled her into him. "Will you go steady with me, Grace?"

"I think we need to take it one day at a time. If you want to get eaten alive, then come to dinner." At her words, his eyes lit up, and she smacked him, "Stop that, you know what I mean. It's your death wish."

"Apparently, I'm like a cat. I have nine lives," he kissed her.

"I've already rescued your ass once, and I'm trying to do it again here, but you're pushing your luck."

"I think you might be right," he said.

Grace thought he meant about his luck running out, but then she heard him say, "Your mother beats mine." Grace laughed because she tried to tell him that. And if he thinks her mother is through with him, he has no idea what was coming. Dinner would be interesting, to say the least. She would have to make sure Raylan didn't corner Robert somewhere and threaten a painful death. Of course, Paul also didn't like Robert, and Gabe had made his opinions clear. Robert would have an uphill battle, and she would find out really fast just how much he wanted to date her.

Before they went inside her parent's house, she gave Robert one more chance to back out. He refused. She took a deep breath and opened the door to a dinner she wanted to be over before it even started.

By the time they got there, all her other family members had assembled. Grace went about formally introducing Robert to each of her siblings and their other halves. All the females were nice, except Raylan, and Jonathan had a tight hold on her. He made sure to stand between her and Robert. Her brothers, on the other hand, brooded as they watched his every move. Patrick and Tane were the only ones to speak to Robert at all. Her father came in late and reintroduced himself. Robert had met her father at the firehouse when he went there to find Grace.

Arlene O'Shea discreetly surveyed Robert and how he interacted with her daughter. He seemed attentive, and he casually touched Grace. Arlene had the feeling there was a lot more going on than met the eye.

{10}

Robert thought he could handle Grace's family. He dealt with hostile people in his line of work all the time. But that hadn't prepared him for the intimidation Paul was trying to inflict on him by his glaring stares. While Bryant showed his disapproval more subtly. He watched his every move, without looking directly at him, as Bryant talked to his wife. But Robert could feel it, just the same. Mack talked to his dad and acted as if Robert wasn't there. Gabe was next to make his presence be known. He came right out and threatened him by saying that if he hurt Grace, they would do more than hurt him.

Ava sat next to him at the dinner table and whispered to him, "They would do this to anyone Grace brought home. It will pass."

Grace was on his other side, and when they said the blessing, he got to hold her hand. He couldn't help rubbing his thumb over her knuckles. Her head was down, but he knew she felt it. Just that little touch had him wanting more. He wanted the right to touch her as he pleased. The prayer was over before he was prepared to release her. Grace pulled her hand free from his as she looked around the table to see who was watching them. Robert knew he would have to win them over one at a time, and Arlene O'Shea was first up on his list. She would be the toughest but the most valuable player. If he could convince Grace's mother his intentions were good, then he knew the rest of her family would fall in line.

100

When the food was passed around the table, and the conversation turned into many, Robert took the opportunity to speak with Grace's mother.

"Mrs. O'Shea, you're a wonderful cook. I see where Raylan gets her talent from. This is delicious," he said as he shoved more food into his mouth. Robert wanted to compliment Arlene to convince her he wasn't so bad, but it was true. The food was so good that he couldn't help stuffing his face. When his plate was empty, he looked around to see everyone watching him. "What?"

"We like a boy with a good appetite," Cadman said with a smile. "Don't we, Arlene?"

"We do like to take care of people through their stomachs." She passed the meat and potatoes in Robert's direction.

"I'm a bachelor," he said as an explanation. "I don't get home-cooked meals like this very often." He put more food on his plate and went to town.

Arlene asked, "You don't eat at your parent's house?"

Robert knew this was going to be tricky. If he told Arlene that he didn't go to his parent's house unless it was absolutely necessary, she would frown upon it. "My mother is not the best cook, she has many other talents, but cooking is not one of them." That was true enough, and that's why his parents had a cook. Otherwise, he would have starved growing up.

"Not everyone starts out being a great cook, isn't that right, Cadman?" The man smiled at his wife as if he had something to say but said nothing. Cadman's eyes crinkled as he grinned, showing his age.

"I don't ever remember you not being a great cook," Raylan added to the conversation.

"Oh, there was a time or two. I made food that wasn't fit to eat. Your father ate it anyway, trying to convince me it wasn't that bad." Arlene laughed at the memory.

"Growing up, there were times there wasn't a meal at all to eat, so you learned to eat what was put in front of you, no matter if you liked it or not. It was better than going to bed hungry," Cadman smiled at his wife.

"We've been very lucky in that aspect, haven't we, Cadman? There has always been food on our table."

"Yes, my dear, even when you had to make a meal go a long way."

Robert couldn't believe what he was hearing. The O'Shea family had gone through some tough times. He wouldn't know what it was like to go to bed without eating. His mother wasn't a good cook, but there was always food.

"God always provided what we needed. We had the essentials, even in the early years," Arlene folded her arms on the table.

"That year we bought the pub was a rough one. We had three little mouths to feed, and we spent every free minute at the pub," Cadman recalled.

"I thought you were crazy for buying that old building. It was practically condemned. But you and your brother worked every night to get it ready."

"I didn't know Uncle Joe worked on the Pub," Mack said.

"Oh, yeah, your uncle made the bar. He's a real craftsman," Cadman said to his son.

"That must be where Bryant gets his talent from. Have any of you seen the staircase railing he custom-made? It's beautiful, it is quite amazing. If you haven't seen it, you should." Macy touched her husband's face.

"Macy, everyone knows what I can do." Bryant took her hand and kissed it.

"Yes, what you might not know, is your mother has brilliant skills too because she redid that entire kitchen on a shoestring budget." Cadman's voice held admiration for his wife.

"Cadman, you act as if you did nothing. You worked your full-time job and then went to the pub, spending the next six hours working on that building."

"Yes dear, but I didn't have to do it with three children fighting under my feet. You were right there with me. Bringing me dinner, feeding our family while you still worked. Stopping when the boys were being mean to Raylan, or when Raylan was beating up the boys."

"You know that's right," Raylan said from her side of the table.

"We weren't allowed to hit you back, Ray," Mack added.

"Well, your mother was the referee, cook, and greatest work partner. She would put you to sleep in the room that is now Mack's office, and when she couldn't keep her eyes open any longer, I would load you guys into the car, and your mother would bring you home. The next day, she would do it all over again. Sometimes she would go over to the pub during the day after she finished the sewing and mending for other people."

"I remember this one time I went to the pub after work," Cadman laughed at his memory. "I walked in, and all three of you were full of paint, from head to toe. Each of you had a paintbrush in your hand, and you guys were so proud, that you helped your mother paint the kitchen. Ray painted from the floor up, Bryant painted what he could reach, and then Mack got to paint up to the halfway mark. There was paint everywhere, but your mother said it kept you guys busy for hours." The family was quiet as they listened to the story of how the pub was born.

103

"If I recall, you decided to teach Mack how to use a hammer, and he smashed his finger. I figured a paintbrush was much safer."

"I remember that. How old was I?" Mack asked.

"You were six or so, and I told you not to hit your fingers," Cadman said as if that was a good explanation.

"That made me two, and I was already beating you boys up," Raylan smiled as she rubbed her hands together.

"Yes, well, if I let the boys reciprocate, they would have hurt you, Raylan," Arlene declared. As if they were back in time, both Mack and Bryant made a sound, gesturing to Raylan as if that was the only reason, she could beat them up.

Jonathan kissed Raylan on the side of her forehead as he said, "Don't worry, Princess, they're all afraid of you now, and that's all that matters." No one rebuffed Jonathan's claims.

"Now that we're done going down memory lane," she asked, "who's ready for dessert?" Arlene got up from the table as all girls in the family got up along with her, taking dishes off the table. Robert took his own plate and started to get up. "That's not necessary, Mr. Newman. We'll take care of things."

"It's Robert, and I don't mind helping clear the table after such a wonderful meal." He watched as Arlene looked at her husband and then nodded her head.

Jonathan grabbed the back of Raylan's pants to hold her back, "Play nice, Princess." The sinister grin she gave him told of her plans for the newcomer.

"Oh man, that Robert guy is in for it now," Patrick announced.

"Yeah, if he hurts Grace, he's going to get a lot more," Gabe added.

"Now, boys, give the fella a chance. Grace must like him, or she would have never subjected him to dinner." When he got a look from his sons, he added, "Just think if the girls acted this way when you bring home a girl for the first time. Bryant, the girls, took Macy into the fold of the family, and they did the same to Julia. Isn't that right, Mack?"

"But this is different because guys are jerks." Patrick and Gabe protested at the same time.

"We just have to give him the benefit of the doubt, for now. He hasn't done anything wrong yet," Mack expressed his opinion as to the oldest male.

"You do know who he is, right?" Paul had been quiet up until now. No one spoke. They just waited for him to say what he wanted everyone to know. "He's the one that got that guy off after he "accidentally," Paul made air quotation, "killed his wife."

"His name is Michael Cunningham, and I believed him," everyone at the table looked up to see Robert standing in the doorway between the kitchen and the dining room. "Otherwise, I wouldn't have represented him. Everyone is entitled to a fair trial, Paul. The police could not make a case."

"That doesn't mean he didn't murder her," Paul didn't even look up. The girls came back into the room, looking at Robert and then back to the table.

"Who got murdered, and I didn't do it," Raylan tried to break the tension in the room.

"I might have overstayed my welcome. Thank you, Mr. and Mrs. O'Shea, for a wonderful meal. Grace, I'll call you later," Robert shifted around the table, moving out of the room.

"Wait, Robert," Grace started after him, but before she left, she turned to her family and said, "You need to make this right." Grace caught up to Robert before he could get too far. "Robert, what happened?"

Robert faced Grace and looked down into her eyes, "Grace, there is one thing I won't do for anyone, and that is having my integrity questioned. I have a job to do. Not everyone will agree with it, I get that, but to talk about something they know nothing about."

"Mr. Newman, can I have a word before you leave?" The voice was from Arlene, who stood back so as not to intrude on their conversation. "Please, give me a minute," Arlene stepped up and gave her daughter a gentle smile. "I won't keep him too long, Grace," Arlene opened the front door, waving her hand for Robert to step out onto the porch, she followed, and Arlene closed the door, leaving Grace inside.

"What the hell just happened?" Grace had no idea what had gotten Robert upset, but she had no doubt one of her family members said something stupid. She had just come from the kitchen, where she had to place herself between Robert and Raylan to find Robert leaving. Grace watched Robert and her mother talking out the window in the door.

"Mr. Newman, I must apologize on behalf of my family. We aren't normally so inconsiderate of our guests, but to say that they won't voice their opinions, is like saying you won't see the sunrise tomorrow. You know, the sun will come up. You just might need your sunglasses, so their opinions don't blind you. I would hope that you won't hold this incident against Grace. She obviously has feelings for you."

"I would never allow something she had nothing to do with affect how I feel about her. But Mrs. O'Shea, my job is hard enough without people voicing their opinions when they don't know what they are talking about. I am a man of my word, and my integrity means everything to me."

"I like your daughter very much, she is my angel. I don't know if she told you, but that's how I saw her until I found out she was real. The night she pulled me from my burning car, I saw her halo. She told me to stay with her, and I saw her in my dreams after the accident."

"I see," Arlene didn't say anymore.

"I'm not sure you do, Mrs. O'Shea. I have a connection to Grace."

"Well, Mr. Newman," Robert interrupted and said his first name again. "Robert, I guess that means we will see more of each other. Just a little hint, how to maneuver around this family, don't run, stand your ground."

"I can do that, but I was a guest."

"Not anymore. From now on, you are one of us, unless Grace says otherwise. Robert, please don't make me need a defense attorney." Arlene reached in to hug Robert as she whispered in his ear, "I'd hate to have to kill you."

He smiled because this was becoming a trend. Each of Grace's family let him know not to hurt her in one way or another. He had no intentions of mistreating Grace. He said back to Arlene, "But I'm the best. Who would get you off?" He heard her chuckle as she pulled back.

"Until next time, Robert," Arlene went inside, and Grace came out.

"Everything alright," Grace asked.

Robert stepped up to her, reaching for her hand. "Grace, come home with me." He intertwined their fingers and pulled her in close, wrapping his other arm around her waist. He loved when she returned the embrace by enclosing him with her arm around his neck.

"I can't stay, I have school in the morning, and I have to study." She released his hand and slid her hand up his chest to meet her other around his neck. His eyes became dark as he moved his hands to her bottom, pulling her into him.

"I'll take what I can get," his mouth descended toward hers, and she pulled back.

"Not here, my family," she whispered as her reasoning for not kissing him.

Robert glanced up just in time to see movement in the window. He liked that her family loved Grace so much that they would do anything for her, but he wanted a small piece of her for himself.

"I shared you enough for today, Grace. I want to have you all to myself." He shifted them, so his back was to the house, and anybody looking would only see his back. He turned her face up to his, and that's when he took her mouth. The kiss was much more controlled than Robert felt.

Grace melted into him, and his mind went straight to having her alone. "Can we go?" He said quietly, "I need to have you alone."

"Robert, about what you asked me earlier." When he looked confused, she knew she would have to come right out and tell him. "In the closet, you asked if I'd been with a man." He put his finger to her lips to stop her.

"Shhh, I understand, Grace. I should never have asked. It's none of my business. I was just trying to figure you out because, on the one hand, you have the confidence of a strong independent woman. Then when we're alone, you become unsure of yourself."

"You should know," she started to say, and Robert stopped her again.

"Do you have to say goodbye to your family before we leave?"

"Um, yeah, I'll be right back." Grace stepped back and went inside.

Robert let out a breath and closed his eyes. Having Grace alone was going to be heaven and hell. His body wanted to get her under him as soon as he could, and yet, his mind knew most likely this would be her first time. It was something Robert didn't think he'd ever come across this late in his life. Yes, maybe when he was a teenager, but now, he wouldn't have thought it. Robert knew he was older than Grace, but not by that much. He thought there might be four or five years between them. When he got her back to his place, he'd need to do a little more talking and a little less touching. Just then, Grace was back with a plate covered with foil and a container sitting on top.

Robert took the plate from Grace, "What do you have there?"

"My mother made you some leftovers, and you didn't have any dessert. Whatever you said to my mother, you must have made an impression on her because she doesn't do this for just anyone."

"I think after your mother threatened to kill me, and I told her I'm the best defense attorney around, so who would get her off? We have an understanding, Grace. I won't hurt you, so she won't have to kill me."

"I'm sorry," they moved down the steps of the porch. "My family is a little overprotective."

"Nooo, I hadn't noticed, not at all," he opened the car door for her, and as she got in, he handed the food back to her. Robert limped around the car to his own side. He only had a little bit longer with the cast on his ankle, and he couldn't wait to get it off. It was the last thing that reminded him of the accident, besides seeing Grace as his angel. Robert still had to replace his car. He was driving a rental until the insurance figured it out. But he didn't really have to wait, and an idea came to mind.

"Grace, do you want to go and pick out a new car for me?" When her head whipped around in his direction with a shocked look, he liked the idea that he could stun her. He smiled and started the car, backing out of her parent's driveway.

"I don't know anything about cars, Robert. I don't think I'm the one you want to bring to the dealership."

"What's your favorite color?" Robert didn't look at her as he drove. He dialed up the dealer to let them know he was coming. It was Sunday, after all.

When he was done speaking through the car phone, Grace said, "I like lots of colors, red, blue, oh I like yellow, but I'm not into green."

"Red, I like it," he now glanced over at Grace.

"Is red your favorite color?" She heard him laugh, "What? What's so funny?"

"There is so much to learn about you, Angel, so very much. Like how old are you, Grace?" He glanced over at her to see her reaction to him calling her his name for her. It didn't seem to faze her, so he thought he'd start calling her Angel.

"I'm twenty-three. Why, how old are you?"

"I'm twenty-eight."

"Ever been married or children?"

"Nope, you?" he knew the answer but liked to get a rise out of her.

"Of course not!" she partially yelled.

He laughed harder, and that seemed to annoy her.

"Why do you keep laughing at me?"

"Oh Angel, I'm not laughing at you. You are just so cute," he stopped at the red light and tapped his index finger on her nose. He

110

pulled into the car dealership, parked the rental car, and took Grace's hand. "I promise I'm not laughing at you. Truth be told, I'd much rather be kissing you." He kissed the hand he held. "You ready to go and pick a car?"

"As ready as I'll ever be, I guess. You do know I've never bought or driven a new car." Grace opened her door and met Robert by the hood.

"You don't know what you're missing," he started pulling her to the front door.

"No doubt," she looked around at all the shiny new cars.

{11}

The minute Robert opened the door to the dealership, the sales personnel fawned all over him, and Grace thought she might throw up. The woman actually opened the top few buttons to her blouse as Robert's back was turned to her, but Grace saw it.

Robert took her hand and said, "Ms. O'Shea, would like to see your metallic red Porsche nine-one-one with the GT3." He turned to Grace and asked, "Can you drive a stick, Angel?"

Grace felt her mouth hit the floor, "Um, yeah, but why do you wanna know," her voice became low as she leaned into him, "because I have no intention of getting behind the wheel of that car."

He smiled and winked at her. *What the hell did that mean? If he thought she wasn't happy about him paying off her loans, he had to know she wasn't going to let him buy her a car. Not a METALLIC RED freaking PORSCHE, no matter how pretty it was.*

"We would like to take it out for a test drive." Robert walked around the car and opened the passenger door for Grace to get in.

"All right, Mr. Newman, I'll get the necessary documents. Will you both be test driving the car because I'll need a copy of your driver's license?"

When the saleswoman walked away, Grace turned to Robert, who stood at the open door. "I am not driving this car, test drive or not. This is not my car, Robert. It's pretty, I'll give you that, but you are buying this for yourself, not me."

"Why Angel, would that make you mad, and let me guess, you'd be tacking that onto your loan that you owe me?"

Just then, the saleswoman was back, and Grace kept quiet because she didn't think it would be polite to yell at him in front of her.

Robert signed all the paperwork, and they were ready to go. This test drive would be for three days, so he parked the rental in the back lot. Robert liked being back behind the wheel of a Porsche again, and he did like the color Grace picked out. This one was a few years newer than the one he rewarded himself for working so hard. He glanced over at Grace because she had been quiet ever since they left the dealership.

"You okay over there? You're awfully quiet? I don't like it when you're not talking. I don't know what you're thinking."

"I'm fine," she said as she looked out the window.

"Uh oh, what did I do now?"

"What makes you think you did anything?" She shifted in her seat so that she could see him.

"You know I was just kidding with you back there. I know how you feel about me doing anything special for you."

"I knew you weren't buying this car for me. One, I wouldn't have it. Two, it would be just wrong on so many levels."

"I can see something going on in that pretty little head of yours. You want to tell me what's bugging you?"

"It's petty, and I don't like it when I'm thinking like this." They pulled into the parking garage, and Robert parked the car in his spot.

113

Robert didn't move to get out. He turned to Grace. "I want to know what you're thinking no matter what. So, please tell me what's on your mind."

Grace shook her head, "I can't imagine what something like this costs," she moved her hand in front of her, "but I'm sure they don't just let anyone go in, sign a few papers, and drive off the lot with a car like this one. Here I am, and my family, as you heard, my parents talking about working so hard to get the pub up and running. Most likely, it took every penny they had to do it. You walk into a Porsche dealership, and the salespeople fall all over you. The woman opened the top two buttons of her blouse to give you a little something extra." She looked out the side window when she said, "See, here's where I don't think I'm your kind of girl."

"Grace, don't talk yourself out of being with me because of the money. You don't think I worked hard for the right to buy myself this car? I can't tell you how many hours I put in a week because there is no time clock to punch. I leave my office and go home to work, and then get some sleep to start it all over the next day."

"Grace, look at me. You know I bleed the same color as everyone else. I found listening to your parents tonight very humbling. They have something I've always wanted. They gave it to you." When she looked confused, he explained, "Your parents instilled the sense of family. You have each other's backs. Just having almost half of your family threaten to kill me is testimony enough to know how much they love you. I don't have that. Yes, my parents love me, which I have no doubt, but, having the tight family unit, that wouldn't be us."

"Robert, that comes from the hardship in Ireland, my parent's parents suffered famish, horrible working conditions, and untimely death. When my mother's dad died, her uncle's family took them in. You see, the sense of family comes from taking care of others when you can barely feed your own. You worked hard, made your food stretch, and prayed sickness would pass you by."

"Grace, do you ever remember going hungry?" He took her hand and ran his thumb over her wrist.

"No, I don't think I've ever actually gone hungry. But, it's more that you learn to take care of what's yours, and family is all that you have."

"You see, I want that, right there. The way you say that with so much conviction, you have that firm belief. How do I get that, and how do you teach it to someone else?"

"I don't know, my parents always said you take care of family. That might have meant watching your brothers or sisters while my mother took a shower or helping get a younger sibling dressed for church. We would fight with each other but don't let someone else come in and try to hurt one of us. We band together, tighter than a bag full of magnets."

Robert started laughing, "Don't I know it, but Angel, how do I get in the middle of that bag?"

"You have to be a piece of metal, of course. Magnets stick to it," Grace smiled at him. That was when Robert leaned in and kissed her. Grace loved the way he did that, and she couldn't help taking in his scent. When he deepened the kiss, Grace lost all thoughts of anything but him and getting closer. She was practically in his lap when they both had to come up for air.

"Let's take this upstairs, or the parking attendant will be knocking on the window."

Grace could feel her face heating, so she knew it was turning red. She slipped back into her seat and gathered her purse and the leftover food her mother had sent for Robert, so he couldn't see her embarrassment. Once they were both out of the car, Robert took her hand and walked to the elevator. He put in his key and punched in his code, and the doors opened. He pulled her in close as he hit the only button on the panel.

"Now, where were we?" His mouth was on hers before she could even think about the food in her hands. She almost dropped the plate as the elevator jerked into motion. When the doors opened again, Robert took the plate from her hands, placing it on the table he had sitting to the left of the doors. That freed Grace's hands up to wrap her arms around his neck as he picked her up. Her legs went around his waist. When he took her to the couch, he laid her on her back. With one leg between hers and the other one on the floor, he kept his weight off her slim body. Besides, he didn't want to get carried away.

"Grace, I don't want to push you into something you're not ready for. So, I think it's best if we just…."

Grace pulled him down and returned to kissing him. She liked the way he held her face to meet his. He had big hands. His fingers reached to support the back of her neck as his thumb brushed over her cheek.

"Angel, we need to slow down because if you keep kissing me like that, I'm going to have your clothes on the floor in no time."

"And you think I'm not ready for that? How will I know when I am?"

"Oh, Grace, I've never met anyone like you."

"Pfft, yeah, not too many of them out there like me," she closed her eyes, so she couldn't see his reaction.

"Angel, you underestimate how sweet you are. I knew there was something pure and…."

"Don't you dare say wholesome because I'm pretty sure there isn't a woman out there that wants to be called that? Like that lady at the dealership, sexy, alluring, or maybe seductive, but not wholesome."

"Not that I paid her any mind, but not all men want a woman like her."

116

Grace shook her head as she said, "The kind of woman that doesn't think twice about showing off her breasts to make a sale. Come on, guys, look for that. They don't look twice at a girl like me. If I didn't save your life and I was out somewhere, you wouldn't even look my way. I'm so not your type."

"You might be right, and that would have been my loss. But now that I have looked your way, I see the error of ways. And I assure you, I'm not interested in anyone but you. The only way I can explain it, is there is a light in your eyes when you smile. You are sexy as hell in a way you don't even realize. Your moral compass is strong, and you've shown me you have no problem standing up to me. You don't know how sexy you were when you marched into my office and yelled at me. How dare I pay off your student loans? Who did I think I was to do that?"

"I don't like to owe anyone anything, and I didn't save you because I wanted anything from you."

"There's that big moral rightness and the fire in your eyes, showing me you're still not happy about me wanting to help you. I don't think you have any idea how attractive that is to me. As you can see, I've been dating the wrong kind of woman. I've always known women to want to be taken care of, not fiercely independent."

"Us Irish have the sin of pride. We don't ask for help."

Robert brushed a stray piece of hair away from Grace's face. "I like my fierce Irish angel," he softly pressed his lips to hers.

"I told you, I'm no angel."

"You are my little angel, Grace."

"I have to get home and study, or I'm not going to pass this week's tests."

Robert took a deep breath, "Yeah, I have work to do myself, but I'd rather stay right here with you."

Grace asked, "Robert, if you're a workaholic, and I'm going to school and working, when will we see each other?"

"You can stay with me every night, I mean, if you want to."

"I can't do that. We both know what happened the last time I tried to spend the night."

"Yeah, you snuck out on me. You should have seen me. I was trying to be so quiet and slip into bed without waking you. Then, I reached for you, and the bed was empty."

The grin Grace gave him had him tickling her, "Oh, you think that's funny, do you?"

"Stop, or I won't be responsible for your broken nose." She fought him off, shifting to the right and then to the left.

Grace was strong for being so little, but he used his body weight to pin her. "I'd love to take you to my bed right now. You have no idea what you do to me." They had gone from playing too serious in a matter of seconds.

"I...I," she didn't get to finish what she was about to say because Robert pulled them both up off the couch.

"I shouldn't have said that because we aren't rushing into anything physical."

"Robert, would you be treating any other woman with kid gloves?"

"I already told you, you aren't like anyone else, Grace. But, I want to make it clear, I do think about you and me. It will be a bunch of cold showers for a while," he lifted her chin to meet his face. "Angel, when we get together, it will be worth the wait."

"How do you know, it might suck, I might...."

"Shhh, there is no way that's going to happen. Take my word for it because the way I feel about you is like nothing I've ever felt. Grace, you've done something to me. You put a spell on me."

"I've done no such thing, take it back." She punched his shoulder, and he caught her hand, pulling her into him.

"Oh, I beg to differ, Angel. That night you put your lips on mine, I was done for. You call it CPR. I say you were putting your spell on me. In the pub, when you kissed me, you wanted to make sure the spell took."

Grace shook her head, "You're crazy, you know that? A spell, the only spell that is being cast is the one you're spinning, like a fine web."

"Just as long as I get to catch you in it," he said with a grin.

"Apparently, it seems like you have me," she watched as Robert got the cutest crooked smile on his face.

"I like the sound of that. Now, when do I get to see you again?"

"I don't know because the last time you asked me that, I didn't hear from you for over a week."

"That's not true. I text you."

"Right," she made air quotes, "I haven't forgotten about you," whatever that was supposed to mean?"

"I'm sorry about that. I didn't have a spare minute last week. I'll try to do better this week. What day are you off from the hospital? We can have dinner?"

"I no longer work on Wednesdays."

"Good, then plan on spending it with me. I'll have my driver take you home." He kissed her and stepped back as if he needed to give her the space to leave.

Grace got on to the elevator with plans to see Robert later in the week. The day didn't turn out the way Grace thought it would. Her routine was to go to church, then dinner at her parent's house, and get ready for the week. She would get her laundry done while finishing up any homework she didn't get to. But, she didn't get any of those things done. With Robert showing up at church, it threw off her whole schedule. It wasn't that she didn't like spending time with him because she did. She liked kissing him and having him on top of her, but she had to keep up her schoolwork, too.

Although he was treating her special, careful even, because of her inexperience, she wondered how differently he'd act if he didn't know? Would he have taken her to his bed, and would they have had sex already? Most likely, the answer would be yes. Men like Robert don't just date without their sex being involved. So, why would he want to just go for dinner and date her?

You know why because he plans on having sex with you.

Robert walked into his home office and sat at his desk, but the work he had to do wasn't on his mind. The picture of Grace under him was there. The image of her sweet face looking up at him had him leaning back in his chair and closing his eyes. *God, I have it bad for this woman.*

He thought about what Grace had said, about the woman at the car dealership opening her shirt, he hadn't even noticed. That would have been something he wouldn't have missed before Grace. He had to admit, Grace wouldn't have been his type as she said, but yet, there is something about her that attracts him to her on a deeper level. She might not be flashy with her body, but damn she was sexy from her cute little church clothes to downright sex on a stick when she dressed for bed last night. Damn, he was a stupid ass for leaving her alone in his bed. If he ever got her there again, he wouldn't be making that same mistake.

He relived the scene when he walked into his kitchen to see Grace putting away the food. He thought of how his eyes scanned up the back of her legs, to just the slightest curve of her ass sticking out of his boxers. *Oh yeah, and when she turned around, I could see her nipples, hard. They were calling me. I was ready to sink my dick so hard and deep into her.*

"No," he put his elbows on his desk and ran his fingers through his hair. "You can't do that. She needs you to be gentle, slow." The image of him on top of Grace, slowly inserting his dick into her tight body, played in his head. He thought about how he would shift in and out of her—making love to Grace, his angel, and getting to know every part of her luscious body. He was so hard just from thinking about having Grace all to himself. He had the feeling that once he had her, there would be no going back.

The thought of having Grace in his life as a permanent part crossed his mind. He had to laugh because they didn't truly know one another, and here he was, thinking about marrying her. Oh, how his mother would react to that. With Grace's lack of social standing, his mother would do her best to convince her not to marry him. If she played on Grace's insecurities, his mother might be able to persuade her he wasn't the right man for her. Not that he planned to ask Grace right now, but if he did, he'd have to prepare her for his mother's reaction, and he'd hope that Grace's morals would hold fast.

How would her family react to him asking Grace to marry him? If one of her brothers didn't kill him, he couldn't rule out Raylan or Arlene getting to him first. Grace had one tight-knit family, a strong bond. Something he'd like to give to his children someday. He smiled at the thought of his angel with a round belly. She was so tiny. Where would she put a child? He was getting way ahead of himself because he needed to make some changes in his own life before he even thought about bringing someone else into it. Dating was going to be a big enough test. He had to make time to spend with Grace, and he knew that wasn't going to be easy. As he told Grace earlier, he didn't punch a time clock.

{12}

Grace got out of her morning class and checked her phone. She heard it vibrate in her bag, and for the rest of class, she couldn't stop thinking about who would be calling her. Everyone knew she was in class, so that made her think it could be an emergency. She yanked her phone out and pulled up the missed call screen. Her brows frowned when she saw Robert's number. He had left a message, and she waited to hear his voice.

"Angel, I'm so sorry. I know we said we would get together on Wednesday, but I have this thing I can't get out of. Call me when you get this message." Her phone asked her if she wanted to save the message, and she hit delete. Just great, it was starting already. Why was she not surprised? She wondered what this thing was he couldn't get out of, or better yet, what was her name? Hitting the little green phone next to Robert's name, the phone started to ring.

By way of a greeting, Robert said, "Grace, I'm sorry."

"It's no big deal. I'm sure I can find something to do on my night off." She said it with a ton of sarcasm.

"What's that supposed to mean?"

"Nothing, except I can keep myself busy. If you have this thing, you can't get out of, I'm sure I can have a thing, too."

"Graceee…" he drew out her name.

"What…?" She did the same.

"You don't believe me, do you?"

"You say you have a thing. Who am I not to believe you."

"I can hear it in your voice. Fine, you will just have to go with me to the thing, it will make the evening bearable. There will be food served, but we will eat before we go because I hate the crap they serve. It's a formal event, so I'll have my person get you a dress."

"No."

"No, you don't want to go or?"

"I don't need you to get me a dress. I have something I can wear."

"Grace, this is very formal. Let me get you a dress, please." She could hear the anguish in his voice as he pleaded with her.

"I said, I have something to wear. Do you think I can't manage a dress and shoes? Unless you'd be embarrassed to be seen with me," she added.

"Hell no, you could wear a potato sack and still be the most beautiful woman in the room."

"Good save, now what time do you want to meet?"

"Meet? I won't be meeting you, Grace. I will pick you up at seven. We will eat at my place and then get ready to go."

"Fine, seven it is. Now I have to get back."

"I'm glad you'll be with me, Grace. Just one more thing before I let you go. It's about my mother…"

"I'll be fine. Remember that mine is worse than yours. I can handle myself, God gave me a mouth, and I'm not afraid to use it."

"Right, and I love t--t ab--t you."

123

"What did you say? You were cutting in and out."

"Sorry, Angel, I have to go," and the line went dead.

"Robert, Robert," *crap, it sounded like he said he loved her. There is no way that man loves me.* And then it hit her, *CRAP, double CRAP, I need a freaking dress by Wednesday.* She dialed her sister's number, praying the entire time the phone rang that Raylan could help her out of this predicament she got herself into.

"Hello," Raylan's cheerful voice greeted Grace, and right away, she wondered what was wrong. "You reached the wise one, ask your question at the beep, and I will answer." Grace looked at her phone and then said, "Ray, it's Grace. I need your help. Call me back as soon as you get this message." Grace didn't even get a chance to put her phone away before it rang with Raylan's ringtone.

"What's the matter, Grace?" Raylan sounded out of breath.

"I need you to make me a gown by Wednesday," she bit her lip as she thought how impossible her request was.

"Grace, just a minute," she covered her phone, but Grace could still hear her. In a whisper tone, she heard Raylan talking to Jonathan, "Baby, this is going to take a minute. I know. I promise to make it up to you."

Grace closed her eyes as if she could block out what was going on. On the other end of the phone, "Ray, look, if you're busy..."

"No, he can wait. Let me get into the bathroom," Raylan's apartment was a studio, so it was one big room, except for the bathroom. "Okay, I'm sitting down. Now, tell me why you need a gown by Wednesday?"

"Robert," she didn't get to finish because Raylan jumped in.

"I should have known it had something to do with him."

"Ray, listen, he has a formal event that he forgot about. He invited me to go…"

"He's inviting you to a formal affair, that's two days from now, then he should be buying you a dress."

"He offered…"

"And you refused. Grace, what am I going to do with you? Why didn't you just take the dress? Never mind, that point is hopeless." Raylan let out a huffy breath. "What are you going to do because you know I can't whip up a gown in less than two days? I can go shopping with you tomorrow, but that doesn't leave you much time if you don't find something."

"I don't have the spare cash for a dress, not even off the clearance rack. Ray, can you redo the dress we wore for Bryant's wedding in two days? That's going to be my only hope."

"We just might be able to pull that one-off."

"Oh Ray, I'll bring it by the pub tonight. I owe you big-time for this. Have I told you lately you are the best sister a girl can have?"

"Not that I didn't know that already, but it's nice to hear. Next time, let him buy you the damn dress," Ray hung up.

Robert put a call into his personal shopper, just in case Grace needed a dress. He wanted to have a few for her to choose from at his place. He was starting to get her, he figured her pride was getting in the way, and she just might not have a dress as she said she did. He knew it was underhanded, but he texted Grace, asking her what color her dress was, under the pretense that he wanted to match her.

Grace: Steel Gray

Robert: Can I get a picture so that I can match the color better?

He laughed when the picture showed up because all he saw was a shiny gray swatch of fabric. Grace was a great opponent, she knew what he wanted, and she gave him what he asked for.

Robert: Can I get a picture with you in that tiny spec of fabric? I wanted to see you in the dress, Angel.

Grace: No, no, and you're going to have to wait and see. It will be worth the wait, I promise.

Grace hoped it was going to be anyway. She walked into the back door of the Pub as Raylan was moving around the kitchen.

"We can use Mack's office. Go put the dress on. Did you bring your shoes?" Ray said over her shoulder. She had her hair tied back in one of her bandanas and an apron tied around her waist.

"I did, but they're kinda plain." She went into her brother's office and half-closed the door. Just as she got the gown up over her breasts, there was a knock on the door, and when Grace turned, she saw not only her sister but Julia and Macy.

"I brought my backup crew. Now, do you have any ideas of what you want to do with the dress, Grace?"

Ava came rushing in, "Did I miss anything?"

Grace looked at Macy, "Sorry, Macy, it's not that the dress isn't pretty, but...."

"Don't be silly, Grace. We're going for sexy, not a bridesmaid."

Grace smiled, "Yes, I guess we are. You tell me if it can't be done, Ray." She went into how she wanted it altered, and with all the suggestions, this dress wouldn't look anything like it was before.

"I'll take your shoes and dazzle them up," Julia said as she put the box on the seat of her wheelchair. Julia had surgery to fix her spine and was doing great. Although Julia wasn't walking on her own just yet. She was using a walker whenever she could but kept her chair close by because she tired quickly.

"I want to do something," Ava said, "What can I do?"

Ray looked over at Ava, "What are you doing on Wednesday? You could do Grace's hair and makeup."

"Okay," Ava clapped her hands, all happy. "This is so exciting, Grace. Robert is not going to even know it's you. I mean, you are going to be so hot."

"I just love being a part of this family," Macy said through her tears. "Sorry, my hormones," she fanned her face. "This little one," she rubbed her belly, "Is an O'Shea for sure, always trying to control things."

Everyone turned when they heard a male voice, "What's goin' on in my office?" Mack stood in the doorway, looking around his small space now invaded by the entire female O'Shea clan. He went to Julia, kissing her, "I was wondering where you went?"

"Okay, kissy face, out. We will be done soon," Ray pushed her brother back out the door and shut it in his face. She was the only one that could get away with doing something like that.

Raylan turned to Julia, "You got your pad, write this down. I'm going to need jewels," she went down a list of things she wanted to add to this dress.

Grace was excited to pick up her gown, but she didn't have any time to try it on. She was meeting up with her sister Ava in just a half-hour. Grace ran through the city with the garment bag over her arm to get to her place. Time was moving way too fast for the list of things she still had to do.

She hung the bag on the back of her bedroom door and went for the shower. Ava was sitting on her bed when she got out. Her sister went right to work on Grace's makeup, not that she normally wore that much, but she had complete faith in her sister. Next came her hair. Ava was working with Grace's natural curls. She was doing some twisty thing, putting in pins and then spraying it with hairspray.

"I don't want it too stiff," Grace said as she closed her eyes so as not to get any hairspray in her eyes.

"Don't worry, this stuff holds, but it will still stay soft to the touch. Not that Robert should be touching your hair," Ava giggled.

The door buzzer went off, and Grace looked at the time, "Crap, that's Robert's driver."

"He can wait a minute longer," Ava grunted and said, "There, you're ready. Stand up and let me see."

Grace stood, and Ava tucked a hair in, "You're good to go, Grace. You look beautiful. Knock em' dead." Grace grabbed the bag off the door. Ray had told her they had everything she was going to need with the dress.

Grace took a deep breath and got in the car. She had no idea what she was getting herself into or if her dress was going to be okay for the night. She didn't even get to see it after Raylan worked her magic. Knowing Robert, he would have backup dresses, just in case her dress wasn't formal enough for his thing.

Grace tried to relax on the ride to Robert's place. She took deep breaths and closed her eyes. Knowing her hair was pulled up, she didn't dare rest her head on the back of the seat. When her eyes popped open, "Jewelry, I don't have any." Well, it was too late to worry about it now because they were pulling into the parking garage to Robert's building. The driver helped her out and took the garment bag from her. He put a key into the elevator panel, the doors opened, and he gestured for her to go in ahead of him. Grace tried her best not to breathe loudly, so she took shallow breaths. The man smiled at her. She guessed he felt the tension that must be flying off her. She turned her neck, and it made a big cracking sound in the small space. *How do I get myself into crap like this?*

The elevator doors opened, and Robert was standing there waiting. He took her bag and walked it down the hall, she had no idea what he was doing, but he was back in no time.

"You look gorgeous, Grace. I love your hair up. This way, I get better access to your neck." He kissed her, and she pulled back like there was something wrong.

"Not now, after your thing is over," she stepped back and turned away from him.

"You nervous, Angel? Just relax. I'm not going to let anyone hurt you." He came up behind her, placing his hands on her shoulders, rubbed the tightness he felt there, and then he leaned in as his nose ran along her bare neck, between the straps of her white top. She had plain street clothes on, jeans, and a tank top, with her hair all done. It was crazy, but he was finding it sexy as hell. Damn, she smelled good.

"Stop that," Grace swatted at him and walked further away from him.

"I ordered us dinner. I hope that was alright?" He went into his kitchen and opened a bottle of wine. "Grace, would you like a glass?"

"I'll take a small glass," she held up her figures with only an inch between them.

Robert smiled, his angel was a lightweight, for sure. She was too much of a control freak to get drunk. He took the glasses into his dining room and placed them on the table. He pulled out a chair for her to sit, and then he went back into the kitchen to get their food.

"Boy, I like the service you have around here," she said just as he set her plate in front of her.

"You haven't seen anything yet, because the service can get so much better." He sat at the end of the table next to her. "Now, why don't you tell me about this dress you'll be wearing tonight? You've piqued my curiosity," he took her hand in his. He had to touch her.

"I think I told you, you have to wait... and... see...," her voice became soft. When she looked, Robert's eyes were dark, and she saw his chest moving as if he was breathing hard. But he didn't move, just stared. She could see him working hard, gaining control over his emotions, "Robert."

"You are going to give me a run for my money, and I don't mean that literally." He kissed the back of the hand he held.

They ate in relative silence. Robert explained to her about the function that they would be attending tonight and why they had it. He told her they were usually very boring, and he'd try to get them out as early as he could. Once they finished eating, Robert showed Grace the room she could get dressed, and he went to his own room.

Robert was done in a matter of minutes and went to sit on the couch to wait for Grace. He made himself a drink and sat where he could see her the second, she came into view.

Grace unzipped the bag, taking shallow breaths. The dress didn't look any different, and her heart started beating out of her chest. Once the zipper was all the way down, Grace could see Raylan had changed the full skirt. It now was slim and had a slit up the side. Grace took everything out of the bag and slipped into the most beautiful gown she had ever seen. It fit her as if it was made for her, hugging the little curves she had.

Robert heard the door open. He was just about to take a sip of the drink in his hand when he froze. Grace stood with the steel gray dress draped over her perfect body. His eyes scanned up the slit in the dress and then every other part until she spun so he could see the back of her dress, and he almost lost it. Grace's entire back was on display. There were two thin lines of jewels holding the back of her dress together just under her bust line. It was cut open below until just a hint of her bottom showed.

"Ah, hell," he was in trouble in the best way. He watched as she moved closer and spun again, he could see the curvature of her ass, and he knew there was no way she could be wearing a bra with the back like that.

"Well," Grace said, annoyed. "You're not saying anything."

"Grace," he stood. "I'm speechless."

"You didn't think I could pull it off, right? I bet you have a bunch of dresses somewhere. Your person," she made quotes, "brought for me." She moved around the room as she spoke.

"It's not that at all, Angel, C'mere Grace." He didn't move. He wanted her to come to him. He watched as her chin came up, and he was shocked when she started moving toward him. He expected her to protest, "I have something for you, and before you get all, "Who do I think I am," on me, you don't have to accept it as a gift if you don't want to, but I'd like you to have them."

"Them?" She questioned,

He reached into his tux and pulled out a long box, and opened it for her to see the necklace and matching earrings. He watched her as he opened the box. Her eyes got big. Those beautiful blue-green eyes blinked a few times before she looked up at him.

"Tell me they aren't real. I can't wear them if they are. I might lose one." She pushed the box back to him.

He knew this was going to be a fight, so he said, "They're the really good replica of the real thing." His chin went up, and he tilted his head to the side as he smiled at the look, she was giving him because she didn't believe him. He placed the box down and took the necklace out, "Turn around, Angel." Grace did as he asked, and he found it to be a win in his column. It surprised him how her doing what he asked turned him on.

She reached for the earrings, "I'll wear them just for the night, and then I'll be giving them back."

His hands itched to touch all the exposed skin down her back, and he certainly didn't want to be taking her out in public because he knew what he was thinking. Every guy would try to get Grace's attention tonight. She was new meat. He'd have to make sure he didn't leave her side, and when he got her home, she would be his in every sense of the word.

{13}

The ride down in the elevator was quiet. Robert stood as far away from her as the small space would allow. If he moved any closer, his hands would be on her. Hell, he had already been thinking about how to get Grace out of that dress. Robert watched her as she stood tall, facing forward until she couldn't take it anymore, and he knew it was coming.

Grace snapped around, "Why are you acting like this, like I have the plague?" Her tight brows creased as her beautiful eyes stared him down.

He pushed off the small handrail that lined the walls and walked around her until he was behind her. He leaned in to speak into her ear, "Angel, if I get anywhere near you, we might not make it to our destination." He could see her breathing as her back shifted, but she held her position, so he went on, "I'm thinking, how do I get you out of this fucking dress." He placed his hands on her waist, and the elevator dinged, but the doors didn't open. "I want you so damn bad, God, you have no idea." His big hands spread wide, so his fingertips touched in front, and his thumbs touched the skin on her back. He felt her suck in, "We better go," he heard her say as she stepped away from him.

Robert waited for a second to try and regain his composure. He knew at some point, he wouldn't be able to hold back. Grace was too damn sexy for her own good. It was a good thing his jacket covered the boner he was sporting. He walked out of the elevator just in time to see his driver checking out Grace's ass as she got into the car. The guy had the nerve to not even look regretful for checking out his boss's date. Robert looked to the side and took another deep breath because he knew this was going to happen all night long, and he couldn't fight every guy who looked at Grace. He joined her, and they were off to this charity event.

As they drove through the city, Robert's eyes kept darting down to where Grace's dress was slit. He could see her dress had opened when she sat in the car because the damn thing showed off her entire leg. Robert's fingers itched to touch her. He made his thumb move over each tip of his digits. Grace must have noticed because she took his hand in hers and rested on the seat between them.

"You're making me nervous with the way you're fidgeting." Grace cleared her throat when her voice didn't come out clear.

"I'm sorry," he took his other hand, closing the gap over her leg. "I just can't look at that without wanting to slide my hand up..." he swallowed hard.

"Robert, it's just my leg. You'd see more if I wore a pair of shorts."

"Oh, don't I know it. When you were in my kitchen the other night, you put on quite a show of those legs. I'm very much aware of what they look like and believe me, it only makes me want to touch them even more." He noticed Grace looking up at the driver, and he hit the button that closed the partition.

"You don't want Charlie to overhear me talking about you wearing my boxers? I must say, they looked much better on you than they looked on me. I liked the way you rolled them up so..." Grace kissed him, to stop him from saying any more, but the second their lips touched, Robert took over. He leaned Grace's head back as his hand cupped her ear to hold her to him. The need pulsated through his body was strong, and Robert didn't want to let her get away when she pulled back. His thumb went under her chin as he looked down at her.

"I'd be very careful using that method to try and control me, Angel, because it just might backfire on you."

"I…" a voice came over a speaker just in time, so Grace didn't have to finish.

"Mr. Newman, we're here. Would you like me to park around back, or would you like to enter through the main entrance?"

Robert released Grace and said, "I think we will make a grand entrance, Charlie."

"Yes, Sir."

Grace looked out the window, "Where are we?" The mansion that stood before them appeared to be a country club or venue for someone to have a wedding.

"This is my parent's house." Grace's head whipped around, and her mouth hung open as she stared at him. "Grace, remember what I said about my mother." He took her hand, "I don't want you to be intimidated by the people or the money that will be thrown around tonight. Just be yourself, the sassy Irish girl you are, okay? Don't let anything anyone says make you think you don't belong with me or here."

The car stopped, and the door immediately opened. The man greeted Robert by shaking his hand. He then tipped his hat in Grace's direction. "Noel, I'd like you to meet Grace. Grace, this is…."

Grace extended her hand, "Nice to meet you, Noel." As Grace shook his hand, she leaned in and said, "Come into O'Shea's and have a beer on me."

The man smiled and turned to Robert, "I like this one." Robert took Grace's hand away from Noel and said, "So do I."

Robert walked them up the steps, "Please tell me you aren't going to invite everyone tonight to come and have a beer on you. You will go broke. You'd be surprised how many people will take you up on your offer." When they made it to the top of the stairs, the line stopped, and they moved up one space at a time.

"Why are we not going in? Can't be there isn't enough room for everybody." Grace tried to look around the crowd.

"They're announcing everyone. It's why I wanted to come through the front." They walked up to a podium, and the person looked at Robert.

"Mr. Newman and guest," she started to write it on a white card.

"No, I want us to be announced as Mr. Robert Newman and Ms. Grace O'Shea."

"Yes, Sir," she handed him the white card.

"What difference does it make? It's not like anyone is going to know me here," Grace looked around, and nope she didn't recognize a soul.

"It makes a big difference to me. Being announced as my guest, signals to all the males in the room that you are not that important and, therefore, fair game. I want everyone in the room to know you are, indeed, with me." He watched as Grace's mouth fell open once again, and he smiled as he closed it. Robert took Grace's hand and threaded it through his.

Robert handed the card to a man standing tall and formal. "Announcing Mr. Robert Newman and Ms. Grace O'Shea," as the man's voice rang out. You could hear a pin drop in the room.

Grace could feel every eye in the place on her and Robert as they walked down this enormous staircase. It reminded her of when she

136

watched the movie, Cinderella. She tried to act normal, so she smiled. *Please don't let me fall. Dear God, please don't let me fall.*

"I won't let you fall," Robert whispered. Grace hadn't realized she said that aloud. Once they made it to the bottom, Grace let out a lung full of air that she hadn't realized she held.

Several people rushed them, greeting them. Grace noticed most of them were females fighting to get Robert's attention. A few males stepped up next to her, so she moved closer to Robert.

"Grace is it, nice to meet you, I'm...."

"She's taken Tom, sorry, but I found her first." Grace watched the exchange between the men with disbelief. What the hell was this, a freaking meat market? Robert took her arm, putting it through his, and said, "Don't let go." He moved them into the large room where people were dancing and talking. "This is why I had them announce us the way I did. If not, it would get a whole lot worse."

"Why do I feel like a piece of meat?"

Robert leaned in and said, "Because you are new meat to the men in this room and a very sexy piece of meat at that."

"Ewww, I don't think I like the sound of that."

Robert started to laugh, "So cute, so damn cute."

"Robert, I need to speak to you before the auction starts," his mother stood in front of them. When he moved with Grace on his arm, his mother said, "She can be unaccompanied for a few minutes. I need to speak to you alone."

"No mother, you speak to me in Grace's presence or not at all."

"Fine, we will speak later then," his mother scurried off.

"Wow, she really doesn't like me, does she?" Grace turned to Robert.

"I told you not to let anything she says offend you because it doesn't matter how she feels. All that matters is how I feel about you, Grace."

"I don't think I've ever had anyone, not like me, and definitely not before getting to know me."

"My mother doesn't like anyone I bring home, so I stopped coming home. I only come when I absolutely have to."

"Robert," Robert turned to the sound of his father's voice.

"Now, when you meet my father, you'll wonder how my parents ever got together. Dad," Robert released Grace to give his father a hug. "I'd like to introduce you to Grace."

"She's beautiful, son. Grace, it is a pleasure to meet you. You have no idea how much Robert's mother and I appreciate what you did for him."

"Dad... Please, Grace doesn't want to talk about that."

Grace bit her lip as she watched the conversation between father and son. She could see where Robert got his good looks, but where Robert's hair was blondish, his father's hair was white. But they had the same build, and Grace could see how Robert would look when he got older.

They all turned to the voice coming from the other side of the room. "Can I have everyone's attention, please?" Robert's mother stood up front with a microphone in her hand. "The auction is about to begin. Please be generous, and thank you in advance for your donations."

"That's my cue, it was nice to meet you, Grace, and I hope we will be seeing more of you." Robert's dad hugged Grace and then walked to the front of the room to join his wife.

"You never told me his name," Grace said.

Robert looked down at Grace, "I'm sorry, his name is John. He was so taken back by you. He likes you, Angel."

She leaned into him, "What's not to like?" And his arm came around her as they listened to one thing after another get auctioned off. There were vacations to exotic locations and jewelry that Grace was sure was real. There was even a car, some kind of old sports car that Robert bid on but didn't win.

He asked, "If you could go anywhere, Grace, where would it be?"

"I'd love to go to Ireland, to see where my grandparents grew up, then after that, I'm not sure."

"Dance with me, Angel?" There was a slow song playing as they moved toward the dance floor. Robert wrapped one arm around Grace's waist and held her other hand. He made sure to pull her in tight, and Grace had her other hand up on his shoulder. As they danced, Robert's hand moved down to the bare skin of her back but not too far from her bottom. She said his name in warning as he let his pinkie slide into her dress. He felt the thong underwear she was wearing. Grace attempted to pull away from him, but he held her in place.

"Now, Angel, you can't expect me not to want to know what you have under this gorgeous gown, can you?"

"Not here, Robert," she felt his hand move higher, and she relaxed.

Someone walked up to them, "I love your gown. Who are you wearing?"

Grace looked confused, and Robert said, "She's asking who designed your dress, Grace?"

"Oh, my dress is made by Raylan," she said, and then the woman looked confused.

"I've never heard of them."

"She's brand new to the scene. You have to know someone, who knows someone to get a dress by her," Grace said as if she knew what she was talking about until she caught sight of the smile Robert was sporting. She knew she had just ousted herself.

"I'd love to have her number because that gown looks as if it was made for you." The woman was trying to touch the fabric of Grace's gown.

"Well, I'll have to get it for you. Robert knows how to get in touch?"

The woman looked at Robert, "I'll make sure to call your office and give you my contact information. I'll be waiting," the woman smiled and walked away.

Robert grinned, "So, Raylan's a new designer now? Although I have to admit, she did a damn fine job because this dress looks...." Robert didn't finish because his eyes raked down her body.

Grace caught the eye of his mother watching them, and she excused herself, saying she needed to use the restroom. She walked directly to his mother and said, "Mrs. Newman, could you show me where the ladies' room is?"

Robert wouldn't let Grace out of his sight, but he didn't know why he was surprised to see her waltz up to his mother and walk away with her. He had a good idea what Grace was up to, but he feared his mother would come between them. Robert followed them to the restroom, and he waited outside the door, just in case she needed him. Not that he didn't think Grace could hold her own.

Once inside and with the pretense of some privacy, Grace turned on his mother. "Why do I get the feeling you don't like me?"

"You are a very observant young lady. Like I'm sure you realized that Robert has money." She said without any hesitation.

"Yes, I'm very much aware of his financial status. He has tried to pay for things, and I've refused."

"You've refused, so he didn't pay for that dress you're wearing then?"

Grace looked down at her dress, "No, Mrs. Newman, he didn't pay for this dress. For your information, this dress was originally bought and worn for my brother's wedding. My sister Raylan restyled the dress for tonight."

"Ah, so the designer you told my friend is your sister," she laughed, but not a true laugh.

"You can relax because I don't plan to let anyone derail my goals. Not Robert or anyone else."

"And what plans are they, to marry my son and live high on his family's money?"

It was Grace's turn to laugh a phony laugh. "I have no plans to marry your son, not at the moment anyway. My plan is to finish school and work my way up at the hospital. Then go back to school to get my Master's degree. I'd like to become a surgical nurse. That's my end goal."

"I have many contacts at many hospitals in the area. I'm sure I could put...

"No, thank you, Mrs. Newman. I work on my own merit."

"So, you would work after you're married?"

"Not that I'm getting married, but I would say yes, I plan on working."

"Would you be willing to sign a prenuptial agreement?"

"Mrs. Newman, I am not marrying anyone. Besides, I... do... not... want... your... son's... money..., not a penny. I give you, my word." When his mother didn't say anything, Grace took a deep breath and said, "Sure, I'd sign a prenup if I were to marry your son."

"Can I have that in writing?"

Grace blinked a few times, "You want me to put in writing that I'd sign a prenup if I married Robert?"

"Yes," his mother wasn't kidding.

So, Grace pulled a paper towel out of the dispenser, took the pen off the little table, and started writing.

I, Grace O'Shea, will sign a prenup if I should ever marry Robert Newman.

Grace O'Shea

Grace handed the towel to his mother, "If I give you my word, it means something. I know not everyone means what they say, but I do. My integrity is everything, have a good evening, Mrs. Newman," and she walked out.

Robert was pacing, Grace had been in there too long, and he was getting worried. When the door opened, Robert could see Grace was surprised to see him. He put his arm around her and walked them to the back door, where all the drivers hung out. Robert was ready to go. He should have never brought Grace here, to begin with. He knew how his mother could be. Once they were in the car, he asked, "Grace, are you alright?"

"I'm fine, Robert," she smiled at him.

"Grace, you don't have to pretend on my account. I know how my mother can be, and I still allowed you to be alone with her."

"Robert, stop. First of all, you didn't allow me to be anything. I decided to speak to your mother alone. I wanted to clear the air, and I think we came to an understanding, and I'm fine, I promise."

"I should have known you'd handle my mother. What did you give her because she doesn't just back off?"

"Robert, can we just drop it? I said we understand each other better now."

"You are amazing, Grace. Come home with me tonight." He took the hand he was holding and kissed it.

"I'm not sure that's a good idea. I have class in the morning." The car was dark, but she could still see some of his facial features with the interior lights. Was that disappointment she saw on his face?

"I have work, too," he was quiet for the rest of the ride.

They pulled into the parking garage and went up the elevator in silence. The doors opened to his apartment, and they both stepped out. Grace had left her clothes at his place earlier, and she wanted to change out of her dress. As beautiful as the dress was, Grace was ready to take it off, along with her heels. Her shoes were so pretty, she didn't really get a chance to look at them before, because she was so worried about the dress. She'd have to make sure she thanked Julia for them.

Robert moved in close to her, "I was hoping to see what you had under this dress." His hands came around her, and she reached up to hold him around his neck. "I do have to change out of this dress." Her voice had all kinds of promise to it.

"Would you like some help?" His hands moved into the spot on her back where he was earlier. Hovering, he waited for her answer.

"I could use a little help," her voice was just a whisper.

{14}

"Grace," he wanted to ask her if she was sure, but he didn't want to give her a chance to change her mind.

Grace said, "Yes, Robert, I'm sure."

Robert didn't know if he should scoop her up or strip her naked right where they stood. He decided to take her hand, and they walked down to his bedroom. Once they stood next to his bed, he asked, "Tell me, Angel, how to get you out of this beautiful gown without ripping it," he spoke into her ear, as he began kissing down her neck. She tilted her head to the side.

"There's a hook around my neck and a little zipper down the side...." She released the air she had been holding in her lungs as Robert's hand slid into the back of her dress to the top of her ass. His other hand held the back of her neck as his mouth connected with hers.

She didn't know how he managed to get the top of her dress open and the zipper down without even feeling it. But when she felt it starting to fall, she held it in place. Robert looked down at her and took a step back.

"Grace, if you've changed your mind," Grace shook her head in a no motion. "You need to tell me, Angel."

"I haven't changed my mind," she said in a whisper.

"Okay, Angel, tell me what you want."

"What do you mean?" She watched as he stepped further away from her.

"Do you want to show me what you're hiding under that dress, Angel?" His voice was so deep with want.

If she let go of the top of her gown, it would fall to the floor. She took a deep breath and released it, closing her eyes as the tight grip of her hand loosened. She felt the garment hit the floor, but she stood stock still.

"Grace," he said her name because he was speechless. She stood before him in just a skimpy pair of underwear. She was still wearing her heels, and her hair was up. There was something about her that did him in. "C'mere Grace, I want you to undress me." She moved out of her dress and stepped up to him, looking him in the eyes as she slid his jacket to the floor. She worked his tie off and then went to the buttons on his white dress shirt. When she got to the bottom, she pulled it free from his pants.

Robert took care of his cufflinks, and then his shirt went to the floor as she stood before him. "There are no words that are in the English dictionary that describe how beautiful you are." He took her in his arms, pressing his bare chest to hers. The kiss was more aggressive than he wanted it to be. He wanted soft and slow, but Grace was standing in front of him, mostly naked. His body demanded him to take what it wanted. When her nails dug into his back, the last bit of blood-feeding, his brain went south. He scooped her up, and her legs hugged him around his waist.

Grace felt as if she had an out-of-body experience. This wasn't like her, but with Robert around, he had this way of making her want things she never thought she wanted, like having him on top of her, making love to her. Although she didn't tell him how great he looked tonight, he was the best-looking man in the room, and now he was all hers.

Once he had her on the bed, he said, "Grace, after we do this, you will be mine." His mouth smashed down on hers, and his hands moved over her body. Having Grace under him had his mind going in a hundred directions, but he knew he had to slow the hell down. He softened his kisses, "I'm sorry, Angel. I'm pushing things too fast." He kissed down her neck, "If you only knew what you do to my insides." He heard her chuckle, and he looked up.

"Robert, you don't think you turn my world upside down? God only knows just how great you smell. You haven't noticed me sniffing you?"

He smiled, "No, I haven't, but that might have something to do with you sending me into overdrive when I feel you breathe on my skin. Grace, I want you so badly, but I'm afraid of hurting you. I know I need to take it slow, but my body is screaming, go fast."

Grace flipped them, so she was on top. Looking down at him, she said, "Robert, we just need to enjoy being together like this and not rush to the finish line. You still have your pants on, and to make this fair, they have to go." She slid down his body until she could reach his belt.

Robert watched Grace as she undid his pants, and he knew what she'd find when she opened that can of worms. If she touched him, which he wanted more than anything, it would test every ounce of control he had. Grace had his pants open, and she looked up at him as she undid his one shoe and started pulling his pant legs down over his cast. Robert watched her breast as she moved, and he wanted to be touching her. She had a thin body frame but still had some very nice curves.

"Now that we're even, what do you want, Grace?"

She blinked a couple of times as if she was thinking, "C'mere Angel, I need to be touching your beautiful body." Grace moved up

146

him, and his dick jumped when she brushed against him. When she was on top of him again, he flipped them. It was his turn to work his way down her body, but he was doing it with his hands and mouth. His hands caressed her breasts as his mouth took in one of her nipples. He felt her back arch up to meet him, and his body fought for release, but he moved slowly and was gentle. When Grace's hands went into his hair, holding him to her, he increased the draw on her nipple. Grace began making noises, and Robert's dick wanted in on the party.

Robert moved to her other nipple and sucked harder as she pulled on his hair, but not to get him to stop, she held him tight to her chest. He moved down over her flat stomach, brushing the stubble he was now sporting over her skin. God, Robert desired her like no other. When he moved to just above her panty line, he felt her body become tense. He said with his lips still on her skin, "This will be so good, Angel. Just relax and feel. I'm dying to taste you. Lift up." He hooked his fingers in the scrap of fabric and pulled. Her body was all there for him to look his fill, but he knew he didn't have long, so he got down to business.

Grace sucked in and held her breath as Robert went somewhere no other man had been before. That first touch of his tongue sent her off. He didn't even do anything to her, and yet her body went flying. Robert moved slowly until she could breathe again, but he didn't stop. He worked to build her up again.

It drove her crazy the way he sucked on her and then changed what he was doing. The next orgasm was harder than the one before, and Grace felt as if she went to an entirely new place until someone yelling filtered through her dumbfounded brain. Robert jumped off the bed.

"Robert, I know your home. Where are you?" A woman's voice was coming from the other room.

"Grace, stay here, okay? Please stay right there while I take care of this." Robert grabbed his boxers off the floor and went out into the living room.

Grace noticed right away that whoever it was, Robert felt comfortable enough to walk around in his underwear, and she had a key to get in. Grace immediately went to the door that Robert closed behind him, cracking it open so she could eavesdrop. Grace couldn't make out everything that was said, but Robert dated this woman by the gist of what she could hear. She opened the door wider so she could hear what they were saying. He said something about them not seeing each other anymore, and then she said they were just taking a break.

"No, Tiff, we weren't taking a break. I was almost killed in a car accident, and you were too busy to stop by and check on me. Besides, we never really worked anyway."

"What are you talking about? We always worked where it counted."

"Sometimes not even great sex can keep two people together."

Grace pulled back, "Ah, shit, time for me to make my exit." She turned and realized all she had in this room was her gown. She slipped it back on and gathered her belongings. Opening the door, she quietly moved to his spare bedroom, getting her clothes that she had arrived in. Tiptoeing down the hall, she wanted to avoid the confrontation, but the woman spotted her when she moved toward the elevator.

"Is she the reason you don't want to see me anymore? Wow, Robert, you didn't give it any time before you moved on, did you? She's not even your type, she's too skinny, and besides, she's got no boobs."

"Tiff, it's been three months, Grace, don't leave because she is not staying." He moved toward Grace, and she pushed the button for the elevator doors to open.

148

"I have school in the morning," she heard him calling her name, but the doors closed. "Oh, thank God, I got out of there." This woman, whoever she was, hammered her. She was too skinny, had no boobs, and was not Robert's type. Where had she heard that before? "Oh yeah, I said it." She knew it was too good to be true that a man like Robert would want the plain Jane girl, the one with red curly hair and freckles across her nose. She didn't have money to get a boob job as apparently this woman had or had her hair done to that perfect shade of blonde.

Grace wondered how his mother liked Tiff. If anyone was after Robert's money, she'd put all her bets on big boob Tiff. Grace didn't linger once she made it out of Robert's building, just in case he came after her, not that she thought he would. This was fine with her because she and Robert were through. She thought how close she came to giving Robert her...

"Taxi," Grace yelled as she put out her leg that had the slit in it, and a cab pulled right up to the curb. Grace didn't have a lot of cash on her, but she hoped she had enough to get her home. Once inside the safety of the cab, Grace relaxed until her phone started going off. She knew who it was and just hit ignore. The cabbie looked at her in his rear-view mirror, and she turned her phone off. She felt the sting in her eyes, but she took a deep breath and held onto her control. She'd fall apart once she got home.

Robert paced his apartment, he knew she wouldn't pick up, but he had to try. Then when her phone went straight to voicemail, he knew Grace would avoid him like the plague. Robert swore over and over again and asked, why did Tiff have to show up when she did? He should have taken his key back a long time ago, not that it was going to change anything now.

149

Robert wanted to get dressed and go to Grace's apartment, but it was late, and she had roommates that would most likely call the cops if he went pounding on her door. No, this was going to take a face-to-face meeting for him to convince Grace he wasn't interested in anyone but her. He hoped like hell he got to do that before her family found out what happened tonight because one of them might just try and kill him.

This time, when her voicemail came on, he said, "Grace, I know you're not taking my calls. I get it. But I need you to know, I was not dating her when I found you. We went our separate ways weeks before my accident. I don't want anyone but you. Please give me a chance. Just so you know, I'm not going to give up, so you might as well talk to me," and he hung up.

He walked to his room, looking at the messy sheets, "That was twice now that I had her in my bed." He went to take a shower because he was so angry with himself. Tomorrow, he'd have the super change the lock on the elevator. This way, not even his mother could interrupt him and Grace. That was if she gave him another chance.

When Robert got out of the shower, he noticed he had missed a call. He hoped to God it was Grace. It was her number on his caller ID. He hit play.

"Robert, I know what happened tonight was not your fault, but it doesn't change the fact that I'm not your type. You know it. Your mother knows it," she huffed, "Hell, even Tiff knows it just by looking at me. I'm just a plain Irish girl with freckles and no social standing in the community. I think it's best if you don't contact me anymore, it will save us both a lot of heartache. Bye Robert."

He dialed her number, and once again, he had to leave a message. "Grace O'Shea, you listen to me. I don't want anyone else. I like the freckles that go over that cute little nose of yours. I like that you are true and feisty. I like that you call me out on my shit. I don't think there is anything that is plain about you. I like that you don't walk

150

around as if everyone should be doing things for you. I love your sassy mouth and the way you give me a run for my money. I don't care about social standings. My mother doesn't get a say in who I want to spend time with. Angel, I have set my sights on you, and I'm not taking no for an answer, so plan on me not only contacting you but…." Her phone cut him off. His message was too long. *Well, damn, I wasn't done.* He thought, how he almost came right out and told her he loved her. Did he love her? He stopped moving. What he knew about Grace and who she was, he liked. She did things to him that no one else had ever done. She made him feel things, like wanting her.

"Well, hell, I think I just might be in love with Grace." He laughed at himself because if his guy buddies could only hear him. They would be telling him he needed to hand in his man card. Chasing after a woman the way he was going after Grace only meant one thing. But he liked being with her. He even told her once when they made love, she would be his. He hadn't noticed at the time, but Grace didn't say anything about him possessing her. He figured that she would say that she didn't belong to anyone. It was almost as if she was giving him herself. Well, in her eyes, having sex meant something more than just the physical aspect. She was willing to give him her virginity. At least he thought she was a virgin. Grace never came right out and told him she was or she wasn't, but she gave every indication that she was inexperienced.

Robert would have to pull out all the stops to prove to Grace that she was the one he wanted. Now that he had made his mind up, he couldn't sleep. He looked at his bed once more, the bed where he almost had Grace, and walked out.

Grace made it home just before she fell apart. The other woman's words kept replaying in Grace's mind, and it was chipping away at her self-esteem. What it came down to was that she wasn't the right person for Robert. If she let things go on, he'd realize she wasn't the one, and she would have already fallen for him. "My God, you almost had sex with him," she chastised herself. "Why would you just give it all away when you don't think you're the one for him?" *Because you wanted to be that one,* that little voice in her head said.

After getting out of the shower, Grace got ready for bed. Falling asleep wasn't going to be easy, but she had class in the morning, so she had to try. As Grace moved to get comfortable under the covers, she saw her phone charging on her nightstand. It was blinking, so she knew she had a missed call or a message. She chose to ignore it because she couldn't deal with anymore tonight. Telling herself, *so what? He had a girlfriend before you. It's not like you never had a boyfriend. Of course, she was blonde, gorgeous, and had big boobs. She was more Robert's type, fake and phony.* Those were all things Grace wasn't. She was true to herself. Her words to his mother about her integrity came back to her. "If she didn't have her word, then she had nothing." With that, she took a deep breath and relaxed. She'd think about it tomorrow.

Grace woke to some pounding on her door, "Someone is here to see you, and he's cute," one of her roommates said.

She pulled back the covers. Man, it felt like she had just closed her eyes. It was too early to deal with Robert because she was pretty sure he was the one waiting for her. Trying to get her bearings, she stood stretched and smoothed down her bedhead. She had tossed and turned all night, so she was sure she looked just great. But apparently, Robert wasn't going to go away, so she went to the living room. Robert stood, clean-shaven, and he looked rested. Why is it men can do that and women can't?

"Robert, what are you doing here at this ungodly hour?" She moved toward the kitchen because she needed coffee, but not before she caught his smile. "I don't know what you find so amusing." She didn't offer him any. She only poured one for herself.

"Grace, I need to talk to you about last night, and I didn't want to wait. This is very important, and I couldn't let it linger."

She took the sip she needed and looked at him over her mug, *God, why does he have to be so good-looking?*

"Look, Grace, I don't want what happened last night to come between us."

"What happened last night, Grace?" Deb came walking into the small kitchen. "I know you went out. Jan said your hair was all done up, and you looked amazing. Well, hello there handsome. What's your name?"

Grace was going to need to drink the whole pot of coffee to be able to handle this. "You guys have fun. I'm going back to bed." Grace walked from the room, but Robert followed her.

"Grace, wait," he walked right into her room and closed the door behind him. "I'm not done talking to you."

She put her coffee on her nightstand and threw the covers over her head. She felt the bed when Robert sat down. "Don't you have to be at work or something?" She asked from under the covers.

{15}

"Grace, I'm not going away, so talk to me," he tried to pull the covers back, but Grace held tight. He started to laugh, "If you don't come out, I'm coming in." He stood, and within seconds he pulled the covers free from the bottom of the bed and climbed in. He heard Grace laughing, and he decided he liked hearing her giggling. "If you are going to act like a child, then I will have to treat you as such," He smacked her butt, "Now, talk to me, Angel."

"What do you want me to say, Robert? When your girlfriend decided to show up, we were in a very compromising position. I thought it best if I left. End of story."

"She's an ex-girlfriend, you wouldn't take my calls, and when you did, you left me a message that you're breaking up with me. You don't think that warrants a visit. Maybe talk about it because that is not what I want."

"Isn't it clear, I'm not for you? I mean, I'm not the one for you. Just because I saved your life, I think you have this crush on me or something. You will wake up one day and ask yourself, why am I with her?"

"Because I think I love her. That's why I'm with her, Grace." Grace flipped over to see him, and when she asked, "You love her?"

He knew she wasn't getting what he was saying. "Grace, I think I love you."

Grace was shaking her head, "How can that be? You don't really know me?"

"Last night had so many aspects to it. First, we went out on a real date in a social setting. I spoke to my mother this morning."

"Oh, goodie, I can't wait to hear this one."

"She likes you, Grace, the way you sought her out and stood up to her. She respects that and something about you giving your word. Anyway, she said you would sign a prenup, which I could care less about, but that's what makes her happy, so be it."

"Yes, she asked me to put it in writing that **IF** I were to marry you, I'd sign the prenup. So, I pulled a paper towel out of the dispenser, and I did just that. I gave her my word that I didn't want your money."

"See, Grace, that right there is one of the things I love about you. Last night, when I was leaving that message about liking all the things about you, I actually realized that I love all those things."

"You think you love me because I did the right thing?" She was confused.

"Yes, because of your moral compass, Grace. You did the same thing last night when Tiff showed up out of the blue. By the way, the super is changing the key to the elevator as we speak. But, the way you handled yourself with her, you didn't get into a fight with her after all those things she said about you that aren't true."

Grace looked away, and he knew she believed them. "Aw, Grace, you can't believe a word of what she said. She's just jealous of you."

"Why in the world would she be jealous of me?"

Robert laughed, "You have no idea what you have," when she blinked a couple of times, he said, "Grace, you are a natural beauty."

"That's just another way to say I'm plain."

"No, Angel, it doesn't. What it means is you don't need any outside help because God gave it all to you, from your beautiful hair and eye color to your thin frame, your strong beliefs, your confidence."

"But she's a blonde bombshell, with all the right stuff in all the right places. She doesn't want what I have. I can guarantee that."

"Oh, but she does, in more ways than one. Anyway, I didn't come here to talk about her. Grace, I'm falling for you, and I will not accept you breaking things off between us." He threw back the covers because it was getting hot.

"Robert, you can't possibly love me. You don't even know me."

"I'll admit, we still need time to get to know one another better, but that's why you can't bail on me. Do you want to know what I think?" He didn't let her answer, "Before we were interrupted, we were about to engage in something I know you don't take lightly. So, I'm sure I'm not the only one who is feeling this way. I just think you are afraid and figured you would pull the plug before you could get hurt. Am I getting close, Grace?"

"I just don't see why, other than that I saved your life, why you'd want to be with me?"

"You are selling yourself short, Grace. You don't think every guy last night didn't wish they were me? I'm sure the thought of taking you home crossed many of their minds. But, I don't want you to think this is just skin deep because how I feel for you goes beyond your outer beauty. You have a soul, Grace, a center, and I find that appealing. You don't play games like most women. You say what you mean and mean what you say, with no ulterior motives. I don't think you have it in you to deceive someone for your own advantage."

"I've already told you, I'm no angel. I've done things that I'm not proud of, like lie or cheat."

"Who did you cheat on? Because I don't believe you'd do something like that."

"It wasn't a who that I cheated on. It was a what. I cheated on a test once and lied about it once I got caught."

Robert smiled, "Grace, how old were you when you did this awful thing?" He had a feeling it was a long time ago.

"Why? It doesn't matter when. I still did it. It's not the only thing I've done either."

"You're so cute," he kissed her nose, and when he moved in for a kiss on her lips, she turned her head.

"I haven't brushed my teeth."

"Please tell me you will come and stay with me tonight?" He made her look at him, "I want to be with you, without any interruptions."

"You mean, you want to have sex with me," she stated as a matter of fact.

"I won't lie. The thought had passed through my mind more than once, but Grace, this isn't just about sex. It's about connecting on a deeper level. If I'm right, you were about to give me your virgin…." Grace put her finger over his lips to stop him from saying any more.

"If I come and stay with you and there are no disruptions, then what?"

He brushed a wild hair away from her face as they stared at each other. "We take it one step at a time. If you aren't ready for more, then we wait, but I still want you to stay with me."

"I don't get off from the hospital until late."

"I know, but say you'll come."

"I'll think about it. Now I have to get ready for school," she shifted to get out of the bed and expected Robert to do the same. But he moved to his back and watched her. "Don't you have work to do?"

"I'm due in court, but not for a while," he put his arms behind his head.

"You're going to have a wrinkled suit if you don't already. How will that look to have the great Robert Newman in court, looking as if he just rolled out of bed and slept in his clothes." Grace went to her closet to get something to wear.

Robert liked the way Grace said the great Robert Newman. "I think it would be worth it. Besides, I have a few suits in my office that I could change into if I have to. I would rather stay right here and watch you." His eyes raked down her body, he could see her nipples through her top, and her long legs were bare. "You like to sleep in men's boxers and a little skimpy tank top." He watched as she looked down the front of her. Realizing what he could see, she turned her back on him, but the back view wasn't so bad, either.

"You have to go because I need to get ready, and I can't do it with you watching me."

"I did see all of you last night, Angel, so there's no need to hide from me." Grace still took her clothes and left the room. He smiled at the fact that she wouldn't change in front of him. It was most likely best that she didn't because he knew what that would lead to.

Grace was back in no time. She had changed into skinny jeans and a white t-shirt. She then put a short blue jean jacket over her top. Robert didn't move to get off her bed. He observed how she brushed her wild hair back, pulling it up. It didn't escape him that she didn't put on any make-up. He didn't think he had ever seen a woman get ready in less than five minutes.

"I have to go. If you plan on staying there, lock up after you leave." Grace grabbed a huge backpack off the floor and walked out. That was when he found himself moving. Robert jumped up,

158

forgetting all about the cast he still had on his ankle. He only had two more days to have the damn thing on, and he couldn't wait to get it off.

"Hey, wait up," Grace was already halfway out the door when he caught up with her. He grabbed her arm to pull her into him. "I didn't get my kiss."

Grace just looked up at him as if she couldn't believe he held her up, just to give him a kiss. She reached up, holding him around his neck, and gave him a fast peck.

"No way is that going to hold me off until tonight," his lips pressed to hers with the force that had her pressed against the wall. When his tongue swept across her lips, she opened for him. When he took his fill of her, he released the stronghold he had on her, but just enough to say, "That's better, now tell me I'll see you later?"

"I said I'd think about it," Grace sounded slightly annoyed.

"Am I pushing too hard?" He knew he was by the look on Grace's face. "Okay, I will talk to you later, right?"

"I'll text you, I have to go, or I'm going to be late for class." She pulled back and locked the door.

They walked in silence to the elevator, and Grace pushed the down button and turned to him. "Look, I'm sorry if I'm sending mixed signals. This is all new to me, and things are moving too fast. I mean, it's not like I haven't dated, but something more serious is what I'm talking about being new. I'm not explaining this right."

"I understand," he didn't, but he wasn't going to push her.

The doors opened, and when they stepped inside, there were other people, so they didn't say anything more until they stepped out and were alone again.

159

"Grace, I don't want to pressure you into anything you're not ready for, so I'll wait to hear from you." He leaned into her to kiss her forehead and walked away.

Grace watched him as he disappeared into the crowd. "What am I doing?" She whispered to herself. One minute, she was in bed wanting to have sex with him, and in the next, she was pulling back, not sure. If she were Robert, she would be confused, too. Grace walked to the subway, talking to herself, trying to reason how she was feeling.

Robert made it to his office, angry with himself and finding this needy side of him unattractive. He had never begged a woman to spend the night with him in his life. But Grace, she made him want her more than he's ever wanted, anyone. He knew she wasn't playing games with him, but that didn't seem to alleviate the sexual need he felt. How could he approach Grace so that she would feel relaxed? In his experience, he would handle situations head-on. But Grace was different in every way he knew. She was inexperienced when it came to men, and he found that exciting and frustrating, all at the same time.

He changed out of his wrinkled suit, and had to get his head in the game. He was due in court this morning, so he tried to put the state of affairs with Grace to the back of his mind. But, the second he tried, the image of her this morning appeared. When she walked out of her bedroom with her hair wild and eyes half opened, to her tight nipples that poked through her top.

"Damn it, I need to stop," he chastised.

"What are you doing now," a voice came from the doorway.

160

Robert looked up to see his associate watching him, "I'm thinking about something I shouldn't be. I need my head to be on this case and not... It doesn't matter. Are you ready to take the lead today?"

"Wow, you must be off if you want me to take over." Lindsey walked all the way into Robert's office, but not before closing the door behind her.

"I just think you might have a better influence on the jury, that's all." Robert moved some paperwork to the other side of his desk for Lindsey to see.

"You mean because I'm a woman," she picked up the papers he wanted her to look over.

"I mean, this is where you're the strongest, and yes, I know this is going to sound sexist, but because you're a woman can't hurt." Lindsey glanced up at him, and she seemed to be scrutinizing him. "What? Why are you looking at me like that?"

"I know this near-death experience has changed some things for you, but I'm not sure how to deal with this new Robert. I don't ever remember you complimenting my work before or the fact that you just recognized how sexist that statement truly was. The way you are turning over control of this case to me, even if it's just for today, screams something's changed. I'm just not sure if it's a good thing yet."

"I'm sorry if I haven't told you how great your work is, but most of the time, my head is on the case we're working on. My people skills fall second to that, and the car accident hasn't changed things for me as much as meeting Grace has."

Lindsey declared, "The woman from the bar the other night, I noticed you watching her. She's not your usual type."

"Why does everyone keep saying that?" The annoyance was deep-seated in his voice, and when Lindsey put up her hands, Robert took a deep breath.

161

"You normally go for the flashy, bold, and blonde with fake boobs and a ton of work done on her face."

"Wow, tell me what you really feel, Lindsey. And how do you see Grace?"

"I see her as fresh, clean, and someone with a center. She doesn't need flashy to attract attention. She didn't seem all that into you, though."

"Grace is definitely different from anyone I've ever dated. Did you know she's the one that pulled me from my car?" Robert saw the surprise on Lindsey's face. "I made the mistake of trying to help her out by paying her student loan, in gratitude, and she refused. She even got mad, came storming in here asking me who I thought I was for doing such a thing."

"Did she know who you were? Or that you could pay her loan and then some, without even blinking an eye?"

"That's just it. It didn't matter to her who I was. She didn't save my life to get anything in return. Any kind of money, she doesn't want it, so in her eyes, I'm on an even playing field with every other guy. This time, money plays no part."

Lindsey smiled, "I like her. She has you humble."

"Oh, she has me a whole lot more than just humble, but we won't get into that."

Lindsey laughed, "Robert, do you know you've never talked to me about anything but work? Much less who you are dating, Grace has done something to you. I like you being a little bit more personable. It makes you more human."

"I wasn't that bad," but when Lindsey made a face, he knew she didn't agree.

"You're dedicated to your work. I'll give you that, but the rest... Well, not so much."

"What are you trying to say? I wasn't a nice person?" Robert sat back in his chair, watching Lindsey squirm.

"Oh, I wouldn't know what kind of person you were because it was all about work before your accident. I don't think we had a personal conversation in the five years that I've been working with you."

"I'm sorry for that. I will try to be more conscious of treating you like a person, not just the job you do for me. I might not have said what a great job you do for this office, but you wouldn't still be here if you didn't. Which, I do realize, is not the same as telling you that I am pleased with the work you do."

"Well, hell, who are you? Don't go all the way to the total other side and get all mushy. Where is the toughest defense attorney I know and love to work for?"

"Smartass, I'm trying to be a better person. Do you have to be so hard on me?"

"If this woman, Grace, has anything to do with you being a better person, I'm all for it, but we still need you to be ruthless in the courtroom."

"I have no intentions of changing any of that, but my head isn't in the game today, and that's why I need you to step up."

"I got this, and thank Grace for all the work she's done on you, without even knowing it." Lindsey got up and turned to Robert, "I'm glad she saved you. I have more to learn from the best," she started to walk out as she heard Robert say, "Now that's just sucking up, but I like it. Keep up the good work." Lindsey walked down the hall to her tiny office with a smile on her face. Robert would let her take the lead, and he was happy with her work.

Robert was on his way into the courtroom when he felt his phone buzz. He stepped aside as people went in because he knew there were no cellular phones once you walked through the doors. The judge would hold you in contempt because he bans the use of phones in his courtroom. When Robert saw Grace's number come up, he hadn't thought he'd hear from her so soon. He always played it as the longer the jury stayed out, the better it was for his client. He opened the text screen to read what she decided about staying with him tonight.

Grace: I will see you later ♥

Robert smiled because he was back on his game. He could now put what would happen later with Grace to the back of his mind and focus his attention on the case. Just knowing she decided to stay with him eased his mind. He took a lung full of air and released it before walking through the doors.

{16}

Robert sat in the courtroom watching Lindsey work her magic. He had never given her full control over a case before. It took him not being on his game to give her a chance. That was one more thing that could be added to how Grace has affected his life. Even Lindsey liked her, and she didn't truly know Grace. It was the changes in him that she knew were because of Grace. Well, she thought it was because of his accident, and it did have something to do with that. It all started when he saw his angel. The beautiful halo he thought he saw, the glow above her head, ended up being her headlights shining through her strawberry blonde hair. Then, there was the fact that she kissed him. He still liked to think of it happening like that and not her doing CPR on him.

"Objection, your Honor. This witness is not an expert, so, therefore, cannot say with any certainty that this was the weapon that was used to harm the victim. He was not there to see my client, or anyone else, use this firearm," Lindsey said with conviction.

Lindsey's objection brought Robert back to the trial.

"Sustained," the judge looked at the witness, "You can only testify to what you saw or what the defendant told you." He then looked to the prosecutor, "You have to rephrase or move on."

"No further questions, your Honor," the prosecutor said begrudgingly.

The judge announced, "Good, I think it is time for a recess. We will reconvene in the morning, eight a.m." He picked up his gavel and struck it down, making a loud sound that reverberated throughout the courtroom.

Robert felt good about today's court proceedings and how Lindsey handled the witnesses. He needed to return to his office to prepare for tomorrow, but he wanted to touch base with Grace. Robert wanted to pick her up from work because he needed to know she wouldn't change her mind at the last minute. If she decided not to have sex, he could accept that, but he wanted her with him. There was that needy feeling again.

It was so not like him to want a woman the way he wanted Grace. The pull she had on him was like something he had never felt before. He knew what it was. She didn't want him as much as he wanted her. Well, it was more that she was unsure about him, and her indecisiveness made the sexual pull strong. Grace had no idea what she did to him, and that in itself was a huge turn-on. She didn't flaunt her sex appeal. Hell, Grace didn't even know how damn sexy she was. How she came out of her room this morning, not caring how she looked. The way she acted was not like any woman he knew. There was no big fuss when it came to Grace. What you saw was what you got, and oh, how he liked it.

Robert: Grace, I want to pick you up from work tonight. You get off at eleven, right?

Robert wasn't sure when Grace would get back to him. He knew she was in class, and he hoped she'd text him before she took her car to work. Robert knew Grace didn't like taking public transportation after dark. If he caught her before she left for work, he could arrange to pick her up. This way, he would at least get to see her tonight, no matter what she decided to do.

Grace heard her phone vibrate in her bag, but she couldn't pull it out in class to see who was texting her, but she had a good idea who it was. She was hoping nothing came up and that he was canceling on her. When Grace went home after class, she had planned to pack a small bag of things she would need to stay at Robert's place. After thinking about how she acted this morning, Grace decided to take Robert up on his offer. She didn't know why she held back. Grace gave having sex with Robert a lot of thought. Seeing him naked for the briefest moment was exciting, and knowing how he wanted her was thrilling.

Grace discreetly reached into her bag but didn't pull her phone all the way out. Glancing down at the screen, she quickly read Robert's text. A small smile creased her mouth, but it wasn't as if Grace could fully respond, so she hit the heart emoji and then send. She hoped he would get her message, that she was alright with him picking her up. As a matter of fact, Grace liked the idea of Robert waiting for her to get out of work. She kinda wished she didn't have to work tonight. But, taking off on such short notice was a big no-go.

Grace's thoughts went back to Robert giving her two major orgasms. Her mind zoned right out from her instructor, and when she was called on, Grace had no idea what they had been talking about.

"Um, can you repeat the question?" It was just luck that once Grace knew what was being asked of her, she answered the question.

"This is unlike you, Grace. Maybe you shouldn't be out late on school nights." Grace frowned. How could her teacher know about her being out late last night?

"It was in this morning's paper, Grace, a nice picture of you and some handsome fella."

Grace had no idea, but she knew her mother would see it. She made a mental note to call her after class. "I'm sorry, Mrs. Jones, I'll pay better attention." She knew tonight would most likely be another late night. At least she hoped it would be. She reminded herself she needed to concentrate. Class seemed to drag on, but Grace did her best to stay on course.

Once Grace was out for the day, she immediately called her mother and then planned to text Robert about tonight. She was surprised when her mother didn't mention her photo in the paper. Grace brought it up just because her mother didn't say anything about it didn't mean she didn't see it.

"Hi, Mom, did you see my picture in the paper? I didn't see it, but I was told it was in there."

Arlene answered, "I did. It was a very nice picture. I'll save it for you. I had no idea you were going to a social event last night. Your gown was beautiful."

"Thanks, Ray redid the dress from Bryant's wedding for me. I got a lot of compliments on it. Someone even asked who I was wearing, as in a designer. I told them the dress was an original Raylan," Grace laughed.

"Yes, sometimes people forget what is important and what the event is meant to do. It becomes who is seen with whom, and what everyone is wearing, and the charity is forgotten."

Oh, Grace got exactly what her mother was saying without coming right out and saying it. Her mother took helping people as part of who she was. It didn't take spending all that cash to raise money to help people. Charity started at home, and Grace knew her parents would feed anyone in a heartbeat. Many Sunday dinners, they ate with someone down on their luck. Her mother would share her last piece of bread with someone in need.

"I know Mom. I promise not to get caught up in all that. It was Robert's mother who hosted the event, so he had to go, and he asked me to be his guest."

Arlene asked, "Robert's mother does fundraising for charity?" Grace could hear the change in her mother's tone.

"I don't really know what charities she raises money for, but yes."

"It might be nice to meet her so we can talk about our charity work, I mean, if you and Robert are going to be an item."

"I will mention it to Robert. Mom, I have to go and get ready for work. I love you."

When Grace hung up with her mother, the thought of Robert's mother and her own sitting down and having a conversation made her laugh. How different they were, but how they had things in common. Mrs. Newman was very protective of her son, as her mother was of all her children.

Grace texted Robert. She couldn't help smiling at how Robert would take her mother wanting to meet his mother.

Grace: Did you know our picture is in the paper from last night? I talked to my mother, and she wants to meet your mother to talk about charitable work. LOL

Robert: Oh, no… I did see the picture. You look great.

Grace: I'm heading home to change and throw a few things together to stay at your place.

Robert: You don't need anything ☺

Grace: I need clothes for tomorrow unless you want me to go to school naked. ☺

Robert: Not unless I get to see it. ♥

Grace looked at the little heart Robert put at the end of his message. She never knew a guy to send hearts in their text. Most guys barely responded with a reply. Like her brothers, it was short and to the point. They would not send her that kind of stuff. They just put what was absolutely necessary.

Grace smiled and texted back, "Dream on."

Robert's response was fast, "Oh yeah, Angel, all the time."

Grace: Later ♥

Robert didn't send anything else, and Grace thought maybe she shouldn't be teasing him. She was so brave when he wasn't standing in front of her. But when Grace had to look at him, and she got to smell his yumminess, her brain stopped working. It was terrible the way that she loved to take in how this man smelled. Then, of course, there was his amazing body. Who knew what he hid beneath that suit? She still didn't know how she managed to pull him from his car.

The second shift at the hospital had its benefits and disadvantages. It was a quiet night, which was good, but it made the time pass slowly. Grace would normally be studying, but tonight, she sat at the nurse's station thinking about what would happen once she got off. Would Robert want to go right to bed? She figured that would be his plan if their history played any part. He had said that he had the key to the elevator changed, so there shouldn't be anyone stopping by uninvited.

When it was almost time to leave, Grace received a text from Robert that set her heart pumping fast.

Robert: I'm in the ER

Grace told the other nurse she had to go because a friend was down in the ER. As she rode the elevator, she kept trying to take deep breaths. When she made it to the nurse's station, she said, "I'm looking for Robert Newman." They told her what cubicle he was in, and she went rushing in to find Robert sitting on the side of the bed with his ankle resting on the end of the bed. A hospital staff member had a Stryker saw in his hands, cutting Robert's cast off his ankle. When Grace realized what was happening, she wanted to kill Robert for scaring the crap out of her.

Robert looked up, "Angel, you're here," he seemed surprised by her sudden appearance.

"Yes, you said you were in the ER," her stern tone was of anger that showed on her face.

"I..." he noticed she was mad. "Oh, you thought I was hurt? Ah, I didn't mean to worry you. I guess I should have said something about getting my cast off."

"That would have been nice," she rubbed her face and moved to the side of the bed to look at his ankle.

"It looks nasty, but I'm so glad to get the damn thing off." He rubbed the dry skin from the cast being on for six weeks.

"I didn't know you were supposed to get it off," she sat on the other side of the bed.

"I was getting it off tomorrow, so I talked this guy into doing it tonight instead."

"Did they do any x-rays to ensure it was healed?" Just by Robert's expression, she knew he didn't get any.

"It's all good, Grace, see," he moved his foot up and down. Then he slipped a sock over it and put on his shoe.

"You need to be careful putting weight on it," but did he listen, nope? He hopped off the bed.

"You ready to go?" As he walked around the bed, she could see he was trying to walk normally, but his ankle was stiff. He took her hand, and they walked out, "You hungry?"

"No, I just want a shower."

Robert smiled, "Me too."

On the ride to Robert's place, they talked about their day. Robert kept glancing over at her, and she could feel the anxiety set in. She knew that Robert sensed it because he took her hand and rested their

171

folded fingers on the shifter between them. He talked as if nothing big was about to happen as she became quiet. They parked, and again Robert took her hand as they went up the elevator. He leaned into her, pressing a kiss to her lips, and she felt the apprehension melting away.

When the doors opened, he pulled her along with him to the kitchen. He dropped her hand and went to the fridge, "You want something to drink? I'm going to pour myself some wine."

"I'll take…" Grace didn't get to finish. Robert did it for her.

"A little," he smiled and showed her his fingers with a small space between them as she did before.

She smiled back, "You know me so well." She stepped up to take the glass he was handing her.

"Cheers," he clinked his glass to hers. He watched her take a sip over his glass, "Now, how about that shower? Are you okay if I join you?"

"I guess we could conserve water," she smiled shyly behind her wine glass. Just then, Robert's phone went off, and he looked at the screen.

"You go ahead, and I'll be right in. I have to take this." He watched Grace disappear down the hallway as he answered the call.

"This better be good because I was just about to get in the shower with a beautiful woman." It was his private investigator. He was calling about some leads he was running down for Robert.

"Fine, I won't keep you. You know that thing you wanted me to look into? Well, I hit the jackpot. I got the DNA of the other suspect the police were looking into and sent it to the lab. If it's a match…"

"Don't get ahead of yourself. Let's see if it's a match first. Great work. Is there anything else?"

"Nothing that can't wait until tomorrow," he said with a chuckle. Robert hit end and put his phone down.

Robert moved down the hallway, taking off his clothes as he went. He could hear the shower running, and just the thought of Grace naked, wet, and soapy was enough to have him standing at attention. When he crossed the bathroom threshold, he could see Grace through the glass enclosure. His body said go, but his mind wanted to take her in. As she washed her hair, raising her arms over her head, he took in her firm breasts. The shampoo suds ran down her body, and Robert couldn't take it anymore. He stepped in behind her, inhaling the scent of her shampoo.

"Did you enjoy the show?" She said as she moved the conditioner through her wet locks.

"What's not to enjoy," his voice was deep as his hands moved around her hips. He kissed the side of her neck, "You are so beautiful, Grace."

Grace turned in his arms, "About tonight…."

"No worries," he took her mouth, tangling his tongue with hers. When his body screamed to get inside her, he pulled back. "Do I get to wash this luscious body of yours?"

"It's a free country," Grace spoke in a hushed tone. She watched him smile, and then she said, "But, that means that I get to wash you." Her hands moved down his chest, past his abs, before he stopped her.

"Now, Angel, if you do that, you might come away with a surprise in your hand."

"And? Would that be a bad thing?" She kissed him again but moved her hand over his hard penis to distract him. She stroked and fondled his massive length, running her finger over the head, brushing away the moisture that beaded up there.

173

"Grace, if you keep that up... I'm...." Her hand squeezed him harder as she moved over his manhood, and he couldn't speak. The rush of adrenaline had him pressing harder into her hand. His head reared back as the hot semen shot from between Grace's fingers.

Just as he opened his eyes, he watched as Grace tasted his come. His eyes tracked her movements as she brought her fingers to her mouth. He didn't think it was possible to get excited again in such a short time, but watching her lick the white cream, was hot as hell. He took her hand, "We'll shower later." He didn't even bother to dry off before taking Grace to his bed.

"I want to take it slow, Grace, but you have my body turned inside out." He tried his best to kiss her gently, in a tender manner. This was something he never gave any thought to, having sex was a no-brainer, but with Grace, it was different.

Grace found the feeling of having Robert's hard body on top of her exciting. He was a big man but held most of his weight off her. She didn't feel as if this was wrong because Robert was the right man. His kisses moved down her body, and she knew what he was going to do.

"I've got to taste you after what you did in the shower," he skimmed his facial stubble over her nipple, taking it into his mouth. His fingers played with her other one.

"Robert, please," Grace's voice was strained.

"God, you have no idea what that does to me," he moved farther south. Moving his big body between her legs, he took what he wanted.

Grace begged again, and that's when Robert sent her flying. Her body's release was so strong in its intensity that she almost missed what Robert said. "Grace, your mine, all mine." He was now over her, lining their bodies. She had no idea when he had put on the condom. He was slowly entering her body. He moved with caution, looking down at her.

"Angel, tell me if I'm hurting you." He slid a little deeper, "God, you're so tight."

"I want you, Robert," she pulled him down on her. The kiss was full of passion, and that's when he pushed all the way in. Grace felt the pain, but it passed quickly. Robert must have felt her tense up. He broke the kiss asking if she was alright. Grace assured him she was fine and didn't want him to stop. They moved with each other until that intense feeling was back, and Grace felt the moment when the orgasm hit. She tipped her hips up as Robert's shaft rubbed on her clit. When her body started clinching, it sent Robert over the edge. His body collapsed on hers, and he rested his head in the crease of her neck. Grace heard him breathing hard as she caught her own breath.

Robert raised his head, "Grace, I want you to be mine."

"What do you mean?" Her confusion was clear.

"I want us to be together," he could see she still didn't understand. He wasn't articulating what he wanted very well for the attorney as he was. "I want you to move in with me."

"Um...I...I don't know."

"You don't have to answer right away, but think about it, okay?"

{17}

The second the words were out of his mouth, Robert knew that he had scared Grace. But something happened when they made love. He knew what he wanted, and that was Grace. The words were right there on the tip of his tongue because he wanted to say so much more than he did. Thank God, he managed to hold back from what he truly wanted to say.

Grace had said something about needing to go to the library this morning. He couldn't blame her for running because if a woman acted that way after the first time having sex, he'd run, too. But this was all new to him, having such strong feelings for someone. He even went as far as saying she was his, like he owned her or something. That wasn't what he meant, but he was sure that's how she took it. God, he was so stupid.

Robert had to put what he said to Grace to the back of his mind for now. He couldn't do anything about it until he had a chance to speak to her again. For the time being, he had to put his mind on court today. That reminded him of the DNA sample his private investigator had sent to the lab.

Robert got dressed and called the facility to see if the DNA test results were in. He knew it was a long shot for them to be back so soon, but it'd be nice if he knew before court today. He could set the investigation in a new direction and away from his client if there was a match. It wouldn't exonerate his guy right away, but it would cause reasonable doubt. The police could get a court order for the other suspect's DNA because they wouldn't take the word of the defense attorney's office.

Robert went to his office before court and tried to get some work done. He had his phone sitting out on his desk, he told himself it was just in case the lab called, but he was hoping Grace would at least text him. The phone mocked him, sitting there, giving him the silent treatment. Most days, he loved when his phone didn't go off constantly. There were even times he wanted to turn the damn thing off. It went off so much. He picked the darn thing up and started a text to her, but he sat there looking at the cursor blinking. What should he say?

Robert: Grace, I hope I didn't scare you off by asking you to move in with me. I just like having you around.

He hit the delete button because although that was what he wanted to say, it wasn't how he wanted to say it. So, he tried again.

Robert: I had a good time last night.

Robert thought, nope, that wasn't right, either. He deleted the text and tried something else.

Robert: Will you be staying at my place tonight?

There, this way, Robert would know if he'd see her, and then he could straighten things out with her. He hit send.

He waited, then waited some more, and nothing.

Grace sat at the library with her books spread out on a table, feeling overwhelmed. She was supposed to be studying for the exams to finish her nursing courses. She had to pass them, and then she could take the boards. Once school was over, she would have a little wiggle room in her schedule. Working almost a full-time job at the hospital and one night at the pub would be a breeze, considering that's what she was practically doing now, along with going to school. She heard her phone buzz in her bag, but she refused to be distracted by it. Whoever it was would have to wait until later.

When the alarm on her phone went off, Grace quickly turned it off and gathered up her books to head for school. It was going to be a long day because not only did she have classes and tests, but she had to work at the hospital tonight. It was Friday, and that meant it could get hairy at work, or better yet, the crazies would be out. She had to keep telling herself, *I can do this. I just need to make it over the finish line. Just don't lose sight of your goals.*

Grace made it through one class at a time, and when she was done, she was exhausted. She had been up late almost every night this week, and when she got to her apartment, a nap was in order. Grace had this special power. She could nap for a short time and be back to full capacity. But right now, Grace needed to lay flat in a nice quiet place and close her eyes. She didn't think she'd slept very long, but when she opened her eyes, there was just enough time to get to work.

Rushing through the doors of the hospital, Grace knew she was in for the night from hell. This was just how her life went most of the time. It always seemed to be a test of her strength, and how much she could take before it broke her. The words she often told herself repeated in her head, *you can do this, Grace. God doesn't give you more than you can handle.*

Oh boy, was it a test? This night put a whole new meaning to the city that never slept. She was pulled down to the ER. Where there was a head trauma from a gunshot wound and a big fire that sent many to the hospital, it had crossed Grace's mind if this fire was set by the arsonist her father had been chasing for months. She just hoped there wouldn't be any firefighters coming in. It wasn't that long ago when she had to go to the pub to get Raylan and bring her to the hospital because Jonathan had gotten hurt badly.

Grace didn't have time to contemplate the matter before she was pulled into a cubicle. A small child lay in a big bed, she was badly burned, and it brought tears to Grace's eyes. The nurse leaned into her and whispered in her ear, "Grace, I need you to stay with her. Her parents were in the fire, too. She's scared and doesn't understand why her mommy isn't here. You have a way of comforting, and she needs that."

"What's her name?" Grace spoke softly as her throat threatened to close.

"Her name is Amy. Thanks, Grace, for doing this. You're an angel."

If she were an angel, she would have never let this happen in the first place. Grace went to the bedside of the small child, sitting in the chair along the edge of the bed.

"Hi, Amy, I'm Grace." She watched as the little girl's eyes opened.

"I want my mommy," and tiny tears ran down her cheek, and Grace wiped them away.

"I know, Amy, but right now, your mommy and daddy are working on getting better so they can come." Grace took the child's hand in hers. They had already bandaged them, so Grace held on lightly, but so the child knew she was holding it.

"Will you stay with me until my mommy comes?" Amy's voice was barely audible.

Grace couldn't say anything but, "I'll be right here. You try and rest."

"Don't let go," Amy said as her tiny hand squeezed Grace's, and she closed her eyes.

Grace sat listening to the sounds of the machines and put her head on the rail of the bed. She began to pray, *Dear God, please watch over this child. Please use your healing hands to assist her outer scars and allow her to recover on the inside. Please allow her parents to return to her. Dear God, I ask that you give the investigators the information they need to catch this person that has set this fire and all the others. I ask this in Jesus' name, Amen.*

The night was one of comforting and sheer pain. Amy would wake and cry for her mommy. The nurses had to clean the burns so infection wouldn't set in, and it was almost too much for Grace to handle. This innocent child didn't deserve what was happening to her, and Grace found herself angry. When it was quiet again, she opened her phone, she saw that Robert had texted her, but she couldn't deal with him right now. She wanted to text the two people she felt had the power to stop this madness.

Grace: Dad, please tell me this fire tonight was not the work of the arsonist? I am sitting with a small child that has been badly burned, and I'm not sure about her parents. If the fire was because of this person, please catch the SOB.

Grace: Uncle Joe, please say a special prayer for Amy. She is a small child brought in tonight with burns over ninety percent of her body. It hurts my soul to see what this child is going through. Please keep her parents in your prayers, too, because I'm not sure about their condition. I feel so helpless, I prayed, but it's not helping.

The tears streamed down Grace's face, this was what frustrated her the most, and she had no ability to change anything. Her shift had ended hours ago, but she promised Amy, she wouldn't leave her. The hours passed as Grace had prayed many times, but when she prayed for herself, she asked for strength and wisdom to do what she needed to do.

Amy's small voice pierced the silence, "Grace, why are you crying?"

Grace quickly wiped her tears away, "I was just praying for you, your mommy, and daddy."

"Can I do it, too?" Amy asked, and it ripped at Grace's heart.

"Sure, you can," she held Amy's hand. "Have you prayed to God before, Amy?"

"No."

"Okay, I'll start. Dear God, Amy and I ask you to keep her mommy and daddy safe. Please help them come back to her soon."

"Mommy says it always helps to say please when you want something," Amy added.

"Yes, it does. Do you want to add anything?" Grace loved the innocence of this small child.

"Yes, I want Frankie to be safe, too. He must be scared without me there to love him."

"Who's Frankie?" Grace hoped she wasn't going to say it was her little brother.

"Frankie is my doggie. He has white fur, and he likes to cuddle with me at night. Even though mommy doesn't let him on my bed, he sneaks up there anyway."

Grace swallowed hard because Frankie most likely didn't make it, but she would not say so. "Okay, God, we ask that Frankie is somewhere safe and that he is not scared without Amy."

"I like praying. God, please bring my mommy to me. I need her."

Grace said, "Amen," and Amy repeated it, and with that, she closed her eyes to sleep. Grace watched the sun come up through the window, and she hoped with the new day, there would be some good developments on the condition of Amy's parents. It was a rough night, but Grace had made it through. Amy woke to the sound of her mother's voice.

181

"Amy, oh my God." The woman was being pushed in a wheelchair into the room they had moved Amy into overnight.

"Mommy, Mommy," Grace stepped up to keep Amy from jumping out of bed.

"Easy Amy," and then she turned to Amy's mother, who had bandages of her own. "Can you come to her?" The woman stood and stepped up to the bed, reaching for her child, so Grace stepped back.

Grace watched the exchange between mother and child as Amy asked about her daddy and Frankie. She told her mother how she and Grace had prayed that everyone was safe and not scared. "Grace stayed with me all night Mommy. She said she wouldn't leave me until you came."

Grace could feel the tears threatening to fall, and she tried her best to fight them back. Amy's mother turned to Grace, "Thank you, Grace, for watching over Amy for us. The nurse told me that they put their best nurse on Amy's care. That you are their angel, and that was what got me through the night."

"I... I," Grace was too choked up to say anything. She wiped the tears that she couldn't stop from falling. All of them would have lasting scars from the fire, but they didn't lose what was most important, each other. After hugging Amy's mother, Grace left with the promise she would be back to check on Amy.

"I love you, Grace," Amy said as she said goodbye.

Grace walked out of the hospital to find Robert leaning on her car. She was too tired to deal with him right now, but when he spotted her, he opened his arms, and she walked into his embrace. After he held her tight, she asked, "What are you doing here?"

"When I didn't hear anything from you, I got worried. I was afraid I scared you off. I went to your apartment last night, and one of your roommates told me there was a big fire, and you were still at the hospital."

"Have you been here all night?" She pulled back to look at him.

"I didn't know what else to do. Once I found your car, I knew you would have to come out sometime. Are you okay, Angel?"

The look she gave him was of sheer confusion. "You know, ever since you started calling me that, other people have been referring to me as their Angel. The nurse told Amy's mother that I was an angel watching over her daughter, and that was what got her through the night."

"Oh no, you are my Angel, I'm willing to share, but they can't have you," he kissed her forehead. "I bet you're exhausted, you want to come to my place, and we can get a few hours of sleep?"

Grace took a deep breath and released it because that sounded wonderful, but she had to clarify that she needed rest. "If I come to your place, I want you to know, it will be for sleep, only." She watched the little smile crease his mouth. "I mean it, Robert."

"I know you do, Angel, and we will sleep, but once we get the rest we need, I'm not promising anything."

"I have to work at the pub tonight, so I can't stay."

He took her hand, taking her to his car, "I'll take what I can get."

She looked back at her vehicle, "What about my car?"

"I'll have someone bring it to my place, or we could just get it later, and I can take you to work?"

"Okay," she was too tired to fight him on the issue. She couldn't believe Robert had waited all night out by her car. Robert was worried he had scared her off, so he went to find her, and when he found out she was still at the hospital, he went to her. This was a night from hell, and once in Robert's car, she closed her eyes.

"Grace, you okay?" He asked her again.

"It was a really tough night. I stayed with a little girl that had gotten caught in that big fire. She was burned over ninety percent of her body. The poor child was scared and wanted her mommy, which I had no idea what condition her parents were in. It was so hard to hold her hand as they cleaned her burns. Sometimes, I hate my job."

"Grace, you have to know that you made a difference," he glanced over to see her already sleeping. He drove in silence the rest of the way because he knew she was beyond tired. Once he pulled into the parking garage, he turned off the engine, and when she didn't move, Robert decided to carry her up to his place. Lifting Grace into his arms, she stirred but didn't say anything about him carrying her. Once he was in his apartment, he placed Grace on his bed, taking off her shoes. He covered her with a blanket from the bottom of the bed. The one his mother had insisted he had to have that no one ever used, until now.

Robert pulled a chair to the side of the bed, he was tired, but he was going to watch over his girl. She had no idea how much she gave to the world. He had no doubt that what Grace went through to help this little girl took a toll on her. Robert made a mental note to donate to the burn ward of the hospital, he might not be the one to hold the hand of a small child, but he could do his part in the only way he knew how.

Grace made a difference in the world. It was a better place because of her. She showed him that compassion and love for life had nothing to do with how much money you had. He had never met anyone like Grace, where money didn't drive her. She could care less about his money or what it could buy her. He pulled out his phone and messaged his accountant to make a sizable donation to the hospital in Grace's name. His next message was to his mother, although she hated him texting her.

Robert: Mother, I want to set up a fundraiser for the burn unit at Mt. Sinai Hospital. I will contact you with the details later.

184

When Robert was through texting, he climbed on the bed and snuggled next to Grace. She mumbled a few words before settling back down. Robert closed his eyes, knowing it wouldn't be long before he told her he loved her. Robert had told her that he thought he loved her but would tell her, he wanted more, like marriage, kids, and the whole nine yards.

He whispered, "I love you, Grace." Yes, that sounded so right. The next time he said it, she would be awake, his little angel.

Hours passed before Grace's mind became conscious, she had no idea where she was, but someone was sleeping next to her. *Oh yeah, I'm at Robert's place.* She looked at the clock on the nightstand. Well damn, it was almost time to go to the pub. Her stomach growled, and that's when she realized she hadn't eaten in the past twenty-four hours. She slowly started to get up when a hand grabbed her.

"Where are you going?" Robert's voice sounded groggy.

"I'm hungry. I just realized I hadn't eaten all day yesterday. I'm going to make something. Do you want anything?"

"I have people to do that," he knew the moment the words were out, Grace was going to balk at the idea of someone making her something to eat.

"I can handle making myself something," she continued to get up.

"I know you can. I just meant you didn't have to." He stretched and got up, too.

"I have to be at the pub in a little while, but I really need to eat something before I go. I also have to stop at home to shower and change."

"You can do that here," he followed her out into his kitchen.

"I don't have anything to change into, so I still have to go home." She bent down to look for something to make in Robert's fridge.

185

Robert knew this would be another thing she wasn't going to like. "I have clothes here for you to change into." Grace stopped looking through his fridge and glanced up at him.

"You have clothes here for me?" She stood and walked over to where he was standing. "Let me guess, your person went and bought clothes for me, and you have them hanging in your closet? Do you have any idea how creepy that is?"

"Well, now that you mention it, I guess it does. But I like to be prepared for everything." He moved, putting his arms around her waist so that she couldn't get away.

"Control freak, that's what you are. But under the circumstances, and only because I'm running late, I will take your clothes. I can get a pub shirt when I go in."

"I have one of those, too," he smiled at her scrunched-up face she gave him.

"Let me get this straight, your person went into the pub and bought a shirt, just in case I would need one?"

"Yes, she had a list."

"So, your person is a she, you kept referring to your personal shopper as your person, and now the truth comes out."

"Grace, don't give me a hard time about this. I wanted you to have what you needed. Is that so terrible?"

Grace sighed, "I guess not," her stomach made a very un-lady-like sound, and Robert let her go.

"We need to feed you," he went to his fridge and pulled out a dozen eggs. "How do you like your eggs? I'll cook, you go shower, and the food will be ready when you get out. How's that sound?"

"Scrambled will be fine, and Robert, thank you for everything you do for me," with that said, she turned to go take her shower.

{18}

When they finally walked through the doors of the pub, Grace noticed her father, mother, and her uncle Joe were all sitting around the big table. There were some of the firefighters Grace knew sitting with them also. She thought it was odd to have a meeting in the busy pub on a Friday night. Her father stood and walked to the bar, climbing on top. Grace watched in shock. She had never seen her father do anything like this before.

"Can I have everyone's attention? Settle down, please. I have an announcement." When the pub became somewhat quiet, her father continued. "I would like to announce, that we, the fire department, the police, and the fire investigators, have caught the woman that has been setting fires all over the city." The crowd went crazy, whooping, cheering. Grace covered her mouth in awe.

"In this last fire, she killed five people." The bar became quiet again, "And we give our condolences to the families that have lost loved ones. But she can't hurt anyone else. She has confessed and pleaded guilty at her arraignment this morning. Please, raise your glasses," her father was going to make a toast, "To all that we have lost, may she be at the mercy of God's hand. The next round is on us." The mob went crazy again, and Grace thought, thank God, she was caught, but the free round of drinks was going to make her job a lot harder.

"Robert, my boy, come and sit with us," Cadman hit Robert on the back as he was heading back to the table. He pulled another chair over to the already crowded table. Robert sat where he could see the rest of the pub. He couldn't help watching Grace move about. The thought of taking her back to his place tonight and running a hot bath for her crossed his mind. He had never thought about running a bath for any other woman.

Robert noticed Father O'Shea watching him, and as people left, the man moved around the table until he sat next to Robert.

"I remember you," Father Joe leaned in to speak to Robert over the noise of the pub.

"Yes, I came to speak with you after my accident about seeing an angel named Grace." Robert watched as the man realized he was talking about his niece. "I was the man Grace saved that night."

"You said she kissed you?" Robert knew where this was going.

"Grace performed CPR on me. I guess the kiss was wishful thinking on my part."

"What about the halo you spoke of seeing?"

"I realized it was her headlights shining on her hair from behind her."

"And what do you want from my niece now?"

"I want her to marry me, but I haven't asked her yet." Robert figured there was no sense in lying to a priest. He heard a commotion from the table Grace was at, and he stood. When Robert saw the guy smack Grace's ass, his body started moving. He moved past Paul, who also was watching what was happening. The guy pulled Grace onto his lap, and Robert felt the rage come from deep within. When he reached the table, his anger was off the hook because Grace tried to free herself from the drunk.

"Come on, Honey, just one kiss." The man's attempts were getting aggressive, and that's when Robert spoke.

"Grace, come here," Robert ordered. The man holding Grace looked up at Robert.

"Go find your own girl. This one wants me." Grace tried once again to get up, but the man tightened his grip on her.

Robert reached for Grace pulling her free, and just as she was out of the way, the man stood, throwing a punch at Robert. He hit him in the mouth, but the punch that Robert threw, knocked a few teeth out. Paul and the rest of Grace's family were there to escort the man out the door, but before the man was gone, he was shouting something about suing Robert. He handed the guy his card and said to go for it.

Grace took Robert into the kitchen where Raylan was working. When she turned to see who came into her kitchen, she saw the blood on Robert's face.

"What the heck happened to you?" She didn't move to help him.

"He took a punch from a drunken guy that was giving me a hard time." That got Raylan's attention.

"Giving you a hard time, like how, and where the hell was Paul while this was going on?" Raylan moved to get some ice. She wrapped it in a clean dishtowel.

"He pulled me into his lap and wanted me to kiss him," Grace said as she put the ice on Robert's bottom lip.

"Paul was on his way, but I was moving faster than him," Robert winced when Grace put the ice on his face.

"Did you at least get in a shot?" Raylan asked as Robert held out his busted knuckles. Raylan smiled, "That a boy."

"Robert punched him so hard a few teeth hit the floor," Grace added.

"You know what, Robert? I'm starting to like you. You planning to hang around?" Raylan went back to cooking as if she didn't care what he had to say, but when he answered that he indeed planned to be around, Raylan said under her breath, "Good."

When Grace had to go back into the pub for something, Robert took this opportunity to talk to Raylan. He moved to where she was working, and she just looked at him.

"Raylan, I know you love your sister," Raylan made a noise as if to say, "duh," Robert chose to ignore it. "I love your sister, too," that made Raylan stop flipping burgers. "I plan to ask her to marry me, and it would be nice if I have your blessing, not that it would stop me if you didn't approve."

Raylan pointed her spatula at Robert as she said, "You hurt my sister, and I will cut you up into little, tiny pieces and put you through my meat grinder." Robert put his hands up.

"Just as long as we understand each other, and you make her happy. I will give you my blessing," Raylan went back to cooking when Grace walked back into the kitchen.

"What are you guys doing?" Grace looked to her sister and then to Robert. Neither said a word, "Robert?"

"I just needed to speak to your sister, that's all," he said as his lip was starting to swell.

"Well, come on, Rocky, my dad wants to speak to you," she took the hand that he hadn't hurt.

Cadman was waiting for him at the bar, and the seat next to him was free. Robert sat next to Grace's dad. He had no idea what the man wanted to talk to him about, but he had his own things he needed to discuss with him.

"I want to thank you, Robert, for looking out for my Baby Girl. You were pretty quick to catch that asshole."

"I'll be honest with you, Sir. I was watching Grace, and I saw the moment things were going to get out of hand. I couldn't allow that guy to have his hands on her." Robert looked straight at Cadman and said, "I'd like your permission to ask Grace to marry me."

Cadman smiled, "Why did I know that was coming?"

"You know, most likely, because your brother told you, but I love Grace. She is like no one else I've ever met. She has a huge heart and a hot fire when she gets mad." Robert laughed, "I know because I've seen it."

"You got my Baby Girl mad, did ya now?"

"Oh yeah, you should have seen her. She came flying into my office asking me who I thought I was, all because I paid her student loans."

Cadman's eyes got big, "You tried to pay her off?"

Robert quickly said, "No, it was nothing like that. When I finally found out that your daughter was real and not an angel, that day you saw me at the firehouse. I came here to see her, and we had dinner, as I'm sure you already know, but anyway, she told me how much she worked and went to school. I just thought I was doing something nice. She might give me a thank you. Grace wouldn't have it. She made me take the money back, which I didn't want to do."

"We can be a tad bit stubborn. Are you ready for that, my boy?"

"You survived," Cadman smiled again because Robert referred to his wife, Arlene.

"That woman had kept me going when I wanted to quit, more times than I can count. But don't cross her."

"I know I'll be chopped up into little tiny bits and ran through the meat grinder," Robert repeated Raylan's words.

"I see you've been talking to my oldest Baby Girl. Now, I wouldn't take her words lightly, she will make good on them, and then she'll call in the rest of them to hide what's left of you."

"Mr. O'Shea, I know Grace's family is very important to her, and that's why I want to be liked by your family."

"Robert, if you make her happy, we'll have open arms for you and yours, which brings me to extend an invitation to your family for Sunday dinner."

"Oh, I'm not sure that's a good idea. My mother is a little…."

"Uppity," Cadman finished for Robert.

"Yes, I'm afraid to say so."

"Don't you worry about it, my boy? Arlene can sweet talk anyone." Cadman patted Robert on the back. "You have my blessing," he got up and walked away.

Robert stayed as Paul took the seat next to him, and as Grace's brother reached out his hand, Robert shook it. All he said was, "Thanks," and Paul got up and went to his usual spot by the door. There was just one more person Robert needed on his side before asking Grace to marry him, and that was Arlene. Robert turned to find Grace's mother, but she was already walking his way. He should have known the woman would seek him out.

Before she could say anything, he said, "I love her and will cherish her with every fiber of my being."

Arlene smiled and said, "I know, welcome to the family. We will meet your parents on Sunday, right? And you will be in church, well tomorrow?"

"I will speak to my parents, although I can't promise they will be at dinner, but I will be." When Arlene raised a brow, Robert added, "Oh, and church, I'll be there."

"See you tomorrow, Robert, and I'd like to meet your mother. Grace had told me of her charitable work."

"I'd like to have a fundraiser for the burn unit at the hospital where Grace works. Last night, she spent the night with a little girl that was badly burned. Maybe I can get you and my mother together on this project."

"I'd like that, Robert." With that, Arlene bowed her head and walked into the kitchen.

He had all of the main players of the O'Shea family on board with him, asking Grace to marry him. Robert made a few phone calls and found a jewelry dealer willing to come to him. He knew it was a little unethical to ask the guy to come to the pub, but he didn't want to leave Grace. He told the man what he was looking for and where he could find him.

When a very nervous man walked through the door, Robert went and introduced himself, taking the man to a booth in the back of the pub. "I want to thank you for coming, and I will reward your time generously."

"I just don't normally walk around with this much in diamonds, but I have what you want." The man looked around, watching everyone in the room.

Robert said, "I need to do this discreetly as possible, as much for my sake as for yours. We don't want anyone to know what you're walking around with and what's in that case." The man nodded and put the case on his lap, taking out one ring at a time, passing it to Robert. He knew the second he looked at the fifth ring that this was the one.

"I want this one," Robert said, and he pulled out his credit card. The man ran it through a card reader. Robert knew this was a reputable jeweler because his mother had bought from him many times. That's why the man agreed to come to him because he knew Robert was good for the money.

As the night was winding down, Grace's feet hurt, along with her lower back, and all she wanted was to go home. When Mack came to her out of the blue, telling her she could leave early, she got very suspicious. But did she really want to look a gift horse in the mouth? Nope. She went to Robert and told him she was out of there. He jumped up from his seat as if it was on fire. *What was wrong with everyone tonight?* Well, whatever it was, she'd have to find out tomorrow because the last few days were starting to wear on her. Raylan stopped her at the door, hugging her. She whispered in her ear, "Say yes," and she released Grace before she had a chance to ask what Ray was talking about.

Robert took her hand, leading her out of the pub. His lip was still puffy, and his hand was swollen. She would put some ice on his knuckles once they went back to his place. There was no doubt in her mind, that was where Robert was taking her. Somehow, she was okay with that. The idea of sleeping with him, and waking up next to him, was what she wanted.

"You okay over there? Your awful quiet," Robert reached out to take her hand.

"I was just thinking how much I like spending time with you. How I'm looking forward to sleeping with you, waking up next to you."

"You don't know how much I like the sound of that, Angel." He glanced over at her as the dashboard lights lit her face. "When we get home, there is something I need to ask you."

"Oh really, it wouldn't have anything to do with you talking to everyone in my family. Don't think I didn't notice. You're trying to butter them up, to like you. You know, you're going to have to do more than punch a guy to get on their good side."

Robert didn't say a word because he didn't want to give anything away. When they made it to his apartment, he went straight for his bathroom and started the water in his huge tub. Grace followed him and stood back, watching him add something to the water.

"Are you planning on taking a bath?" She questioned.

"Nope, you are. I'm sure after the last few days, you could use one to relax, soak a little."

"You're running a bath just for me? You don't plan on joining me?"

"Nope, I want this to be about you, and we both know what would happen if I got in with you. You go ahead and get in. I'll bring you a glass of wine." He did the one inch with his fingers, and she smiled at him. "Such a lightweight," he said as he walked out.

Grace watched him go. This man confused her in so many ways. He was running her a bubble bath and getting her a glass of wine. What man does things like that? *One that wants to take care of you, Grace?* She undressed and stepped into the hot water. She couldn't stop the sound that escaped her lips. Her body sunk deep into the tub and her eyes closed. She turned off the water with her toes.

Robert walked back into the room, and just the sight of her relaxing in that big tub that no one ever used gave him joy. "Feel good?" He asked to let her know he was there.

"It feels great, and you won't join me?" She never even opened her eyes.

"I'll just watch if that's okay with you. The tub has jets. You want me to put them on?"

"Oh, if you do that, I will never get out." He pushed a few buttons on the side of the tub, and the light bubbling sound rumbled through the water. "OH… MY…God, Robert, I love you." She said in a dreamy voice.

"I love you, too, Grace," he leaned against the edge of the tub. When her eyes opened, he asked her what he'd wanted to ask all night. "Grace, I'd be honored if you'd marry me. You don't have to answer right now. I know you might need more time."

He held the box open for her to see the ring he had picked out for her. She scooted up in the tub as her eyes became big.

"You're serious, oh, Robert. Is that what you talked to my family about? Oh, oh, you even talked to Raylan. That's why she whispered in my ear to say yes." She forgot all about being in the tub and jumped into his arms. Even though he wasn't prepared for her, he didn't drop her. Her wet body soaked his shirt as she wrapped her legs around him.

"Does this mean you'll marry me, Angel? You have to tell me."

"YES! YES!" she shouted in his ear. "Oh, sorry," and she kissed the good side of his mouth. He walked with her wrapped around him to the bed. When he placed her in the center, he took the ring out of the box, sliding it on her slender left ring finger.

"It might need to be sized, but I didn't want to wait to give it to you."

"It's beautiful but so big," she held up her hand. "I can't believe you want to marry me." She joked with him, "I'm so not your type."

He playfully smacked the side of her butt, "That's because I was dating the wrong type, to begin with. It took you to show me what I should have been looking for all along. I love you, Grace, my Angel. You are so mine. You hear me, mine, mine, mine, you are all mine."

Grace laughed at Robert's antics, but she kinda liked being his. When Robert moved closer to her face, he whispered, "I love you," and closed the short distance between them. Robert recoiled when their lips touched. He had forgotten about his busted lip.

"Maybe we should bypass kissing for tonight," Grace smiled up at him.

"I hate that idea," and he softly kissed her. She was naked from her bath, and he was still fully clothed. He started to remove his clothes, one item at a time, as they hit the floor. He slipped on a condom to protect them. He couldn't wait until his body was touching hers.

196

"You are mine, Angel," he said in a soft, tender voice as he entered her.

"Yes, I am," she replied as her body began to move with his. "I love you, Robert Newman. I'm so glad you got thrown right in front of me."

"I'm glad I have an angel on my side." The talk ended when the pleasure began to build. Robert reached between Grace's legs and found the tight bundle of nerves that sent her over the edge, and he followed. They stayed intertwined for a long time before Grace spoke.

"You do know what you're getting yourself into by marrying me, right?"

"Yes, I do."

"You marry me, then you marry my family."

"Grace, you are not talking me out of marrying you, and if I have to put up with yours, then you have to do the same when it comes to mine."

"Oh, right, your mother. Does she know? Holy crap, she is not going to like it. You might want to rethink this," Robert kissed her words away. There was nothing that would stop him from marrying Grace.

"Not a chance," and Robert kissed her some more, even with his lip hurting like hell. He loved being with Grace.

Epilogue

The next morning, Robert wanted to put off calling his mother for as long as he could, but Arlene was expecting his parents to be at Sunday dinner. So, not only did he have to tell her that he proposed to Grace and that she accepted, but they needed to be at a dinner with her entire family. Well, he couldn't put it off any longer.

Robert took a deep breath and dialed his mother, "Hello, Mother."

"Oh, Robert dear, are you calling about the message you left me last night." His mother sounded as if she was in a good mood, and Robert thought, not for long.

"Um, not really, but I have news and an extended invitation. I need you to be calm and hear me out before you say…."

"Robert, what have you done?" Now his mother's voice became concerned.

"Mother, I asked Grace to marry me, and she accepted." Robert expected his mother to yell or for her to be angry, but there was only silence on the other end of the phone, "Mother?"

"I heard you, Robert. So, Grace is the one you want to spend the rest of your life with?" Her tone was tight, as if she was holding back what she truly wanted to say.

"Yes, Mother, I love Grace, and she loves me."

"What's not to love? You have already presented her with a ring, I assume?"

"Yes, I have, and just so you know, the ring is small to your standards, but the ring is about what Grace would like and not about how people perceive Robert Newman's reputation. She doesn't want my money. She wants me. Do you have any idea how great that feels? She fights me every time I even attempt to spend any money on her."

"Yes, well, she is someone that might be lacking breeding, but she makes up for it with high morals. Now, you said something about an invitation?"

"Grace's parents have invited you and Dad for Sunday dinner. It's a big thing at her house. So, I would like you to make every effort to be there. And Mom, I need you to be on your best behavior. This is important to me."

"I don't think I need my child to tell me how to act. Where will this dinner take place?"

Robert heard his father in the background, "We'll be there, son. Text me the address, and I'll have your mother there with her shock collar on."

"John, I don't think that comment was necessary." Robert started to laugh because his parents were like night and day.

Grace came out of the bathroom and asked, "How did it go with your mother?" She walked over to the closet and looked through the dresses Robert had bought her for church.

When he came up behind her, wrapping his arms around her waist, he said, "As well as expected, but she really doesn't have a say. I made my choice, and she has to live with it because nothing will change my mind about you."

"And what about dinner at my parent's house? How did that go over?" Grace continued moving through the clothes.

Robert chuckled, "My father said they will be there, and he'd make sure my mother wore her shock collar."

Grace began to laugh when she said, "He did not say that."

"He did, and I have no idea how my parents ever managed to get married. They are complete opposites, but they love each other."

"Can I ask, although I think I know the answer, who had the money, your mother or dad?"

"Mom's family had more money than my fathers, but his family wasn't poor, by any means."

"Like my parents, you would never know they had money. They worked hard to get where they are now, but they always give to the needy because at one time they were the ones in need."

"I think my dad will get along with yours just fine, but my mother can be a lot of work."

"Don't worry about it. My mom wants to talk to yours about charitable work. They have that in common, although they go about it differently."

"Speaking of that, I did something. I donated money to the burn unit in your name. I know seeing that young girl last night was hard on you, and I couldn't think of a better way to spend money than to help young burn victims."

"Oh, Robert," Grace hugged him. "I love that idea," she gently kissed his less swollen lip.

"I also want to get our mothers together on a fundraiser for the burn unit. Both of them are on board."

"You talked to my mother about this. I mean, about working with your mother?" The surprise was apparent on Grace's face.

"Yes, Angel, I did," that earned him Grace, pressing her lips to his as she backed him up to the edge of the bed. "We're going to be late for church, Grace."

Grace and Robert walked through the doors of the church just as they were being closed. They quickly sat on the outside edge of the first pew her family always sat in, so they didn't draw her mother's attention. However, Grace knew she would have something to say after the service.

Raylan nudged Robert, and when he looked at her, she wanted him to get her sister's attention. Robert then tapped Grace. When she looked over, Raylan pointed to her ring on her left hand. Grace discreetly held up her left hand to show Raylan her engagement ring. Raylan snatched Grace's hand over Robert's lap so she could look at it. That, in turn, drew Ava's attention, she was leaning over to see the ring when Arlene cleared her throat, and everyone went back to sitting straight in their seats.

After church, the girls in the family swarmed Grace, all wanting to see her ring. They all talked at once, and Grace looked up to see Robert watching her. She smiled at him. His eyes said it all, the intense stare, and he mouthed "I love you," and Grace's heart skipped a beat. She thanked God for putting this man in her path.

Back at her parent's house, Grace could feel the tension building. Robert's parents hadn't shown up yet, and Grace knew how her mother felt about punctuality. It was rude to show up late when you were invited for dinner, she always said. Robert must have noticed because he came to her, putting his arms around her.

"They are on their way. My father messaged me a little while ago. I'm sure they will be here any minute."

"I just know how my mother can be about guests being late for dinner." The doorbell rang, and Grace released a deep sigh. Robert kissed her forehead.

When Robert's parents came into the house, Grace could see Robert's mother look around. But his father made a b-line for her, taking her from Robert to hug her. Grace stepped up to do the introduction.

"Mom, Dad, this is Helen and John Newman. Helen, John, these are my parents, Arlene and Cadman O'Shea." Everyone shook hands, and Arlene ushered the newcomers into the living room. Grace watched as her family members looked in but kept moving, and she wished she could go with them. She couldn't remember ever feeling uncomfortable in her childhood home.

Robert's mother and Arlene talked about the different charities they gave their time to. While John and her father talked about the firehouse and the new developments with the most recent fire. Grace relaxed a little when Robert pulled her into him. She took comfort in his scent, and he noticed as the one side of his mouth went up. Grace thought, how did she get so lucky?

Arlene asked Helen if she'd like to help in the kitchen, and Robert chuckled in Grace's ear as he said, "I wonder how that will go?"

Once everyone was seated in the dining room, and the food was on the table, Arlene asked everyone to hold hands to say the blessing.

As the food was passed, Helen looked around the table. "You have a large family, Grace."

"Oh, excuse my manners," Grace stood, "Let me introduce my family. Next to my father is my oldest brother, Mack, and next to him is his fiancée, Julia Mealey. Julia had back surgery a few months ago to repair her severed spine that she suffered from a car accident."

"Bryant is the next to the oldest in the O'Shea family, and Macy," with the mention of her name, Macy did a little wave. "She is Bryant's wife, and they are expecting their first child." Grace put out her hand in Raylan's direction on the other side of the table. "On my father's other side is my oldest sister Raylan, she runs the kitchen at the pub, and if you ever get a chance, you must try her food. Anyway, this is Jonathan, who is waiting patiently to marry my sister. He works with my father at the firehouse. Next to them is my brother Paul, who is also a firefighter, then my younger twin brothers, Patrick and Gabe, who are in college. Ava is my little sister, who goes to school, too, and then there's Tane, who's in high school. Everyone, these are Robert's parents, Helen and John." Grace sat back down.

"Wow," John said as he turned to Raylan. "Raylan, that's such a pretty name. I've heard about you. You're the one who makes a big deal on St. Patrick's Day, right?"

"That would be me," Raylan was surprised that he would have heard about her food.

"When is the wedding?"

Jonathan looked over at her and said, "Yes, Princess, when are you going to marry me? If things don't start moving along, I swear I'm going to have to take matters into my own hands."

Paul was talking to his father about something going on at the firehouse. "I don't want to do it this year. It's so lame to have a male photographer take pictures for a hot firefighter calendar."

"I have to agree," Jonathan added when Raylan just waved him off about setting a date for their wedding.

"You boys know we make a lot of money off those calendars, money the firehouse needs to buy equipment we can't get from city funds."

"Yeah, but it wouldn't hurt if we actually had a female to take the pictures. I think the guys would be more likely to do it."

"I think if it makes the calendar better, you might want to consider it, Cadman." Arlene put her two cents in.

Helen spoke up, "I know someone that could take the pictures. She's cute, too."

"See, was that so hard, Dad? Mrs. Newman knows a cute photographer?"

"I might be able to sell some of those calendars for you, too. I have many groups of women that go for that kind of stuff."

"Thank you, Helen. I would like to get that number for the photographer," Cadman smiled at his wife.

When his dad had agreed to go with a female to take the pictures, Paul started thinking about what he'd wear to the photoshoot. He knew he would enjoy this year's calendar.

Watch out for Lucky Shot!

Find Trish Collins on the web.

Facebook

Instagram

Trishcollinsauthor.net

TrishCollins.Author@gmail.com

Amazon.com

For free goodies, mail a self-addressed stamped envelope to:

Trish Collins

P.O. Box 695

Warrenville, S.C.

29841

While supplies last!

Keep reading for a sneak peek of b

Breaking Waves of Love

Book 3 in the Jacobs Series.

~1~

Dannie Jacobs knew what her mother was up to, but here she was, delivering leftover food to Leo Waiholua. He was one of the surf shop's newest employees. Her mother had planned a big holiday meal, and she expected everyone to attend. Leo didn't get the memo that these things weren't optional. When Linda Jacobs took you in as one of her family members, there was no getting out. It was much like the Mafia. Once you're in, you're in for life. Leo had told her mother he had other plans and couldn't make it. Do you think that would deter Linda from trying to push her and Leo together? No such luck?

Dannie was taking a break from men. After finding her ex-boss and boyfriend cheating on her, she didn't have a fond opinion of the male species right now. Dannie was putting all her attention toward revamping the surf shop's website. This was what she did for a major company in Texas before she quit her job. At first, she wasn't happy about returning home, but she was now looking forward to putting her own stamp on the shop.

Dannie looked down at the piece of paper in her hand with Leo's address on it. She tried to put it into her GPS, but it said the address didn't exist. So, either he gave a bogus address or was invisible because she had been up and down the street and couldn't find him. She pulled over by the closest house to the number of his place. Getting out of her van, she felt like an idiot carrying all this food and not knowing where she was going. As she walked down the sidewalk, she saw a small sign with Leo's house number on it. There was a brick walkway. Dannie took a deep breath and followed it. It went down the side of a house, and she came to a garage. On the door, it had the number she had been looking for.

Dannie stood there debating to put the food down, knock, then run. What was she, five? Dannie rapped on the door, stood back, and waited. There was a noise inside, and she knew the door was about to open. When Leo stood there shirtless, his long hair down, and in pair of board shorts, she couldn't speak. He rested his arm on the door jam, waiting for her to say something. But she couldn't because there was no saliva in her mouth. There was a whole lot of his caramel skin on display, along with a dark black tat that covered his shoulder and went down his arm.

"What are you doing here?" He was shocked to see Dannie standing at his door, in a dress no less, and her hair long. She just stood there looking at him, and the way she stared had his body stirring.

"I... I, um. My mother sent you leftovers." Dannie shoved the food in her hands out for him to take.

He didn't move to take the food. It was his turn to survey Dannie up and down, and she could feel her heart beating faster. Her eyes darted down away from his face. He had a patch of black curly hair between his very nice defined pecs that went down past. He snapped his fingers in front of her face, and she jerked her eyes up to his.

"I'm up here, Dannie," he put one arm out to take the containers out of her hands. She just remained where she was, not moving to leave. There was an awkward moment where neither one moved or said a word. When it went on too long, Leo spoke first, "Dannie, you need to go. Thank your mother for the food." He shut the door with her still standing there, stunned.

Dannie shook off the stupor she was in and then got mad. *How dare he shut the door in my face. You are an idiot, Danielle Jacobs.* She marched back down the path to her van, berating herself the entire way. *Well, what did you expect him to do? You just stood there staring at his bare chest, the one you are not interested in. Yeah, right, you can lie to everyone else, oh, but you can't lie to me.* Dannie stomped her feet as she went the last stretch and shook her head. Now not only was she talking to herself, but she was answering, too. She got into her van and slammed the door.

~ ~ ~ ~ ~ ~

Leo tossed the food containers onto the workbench that he used as a counter. He leaned his back against it, looking at the place he called home. Leo slept on a mattress on the floor and the bathroom without a door. Home sweet home, he thought. He hoped like hell Dannie couldn't see inside. The way she stood there looking at him had him thinking about dragging her inside and...

"Nope, don't go there. You did the right thing by telling her to go." Leo headed to the shower. It would be a cold one if he couldn't get the image of Dannie in that short red dress out of his head. He stepped into the small stall and leaned his head on the wall letting the water run over it. "She doesn't want you, dude. So, stop thinking about her and move on." But the way she looked at him said something different. "Until she admits to wanting you, you have to back off." He laughed at the advice he was giving himself.

The thought of her long hair hanging down her back, free to get his fingers tangled in as he kissed her. How would her body feel pressed against his? He'd love to roll her under him, and... "Shit," he was doing it again, fantasizing about her. The cold water wasn't helping, so he did the one thing that would finish him off. He soaped up his hands, stroking his hard dick, and thought about Dannie standing naked in front of him.

His eyes roamed over her body, her big round tits, and he guessed she would have dark nipples. How would they fit into his large hands? He could see how her nipple would harden for him when he touched them. Man, he wanted to get his mouth on her, suck her deep and hard. Make her squirm with pleasure, oh yeah. Then he would move down her body, loving every inch of her, until he got to the heart of her. He'd spread her wide so he could taste her juices.

That was all it took as his hand moved faster and squeezed his shaft. The hot, white cream shot out as his head flew back. The release was hard and satisfying. Without physically being with her, it was the best he could do.

~ ~ ~ ~ ~ ~

Dannie pulled her van into the back lot of the surf shop. She had moved into her brother Ben's third-floor apartment over the shop, when he bought Liz the house. Liz had come to California to do some research for a book she was writing and fell in love with her brother. They were married now and just had a set of twins and her step-niece Paige. Dannie smiled at the thought of her new little niece and nephew. Kenneth and Sophie were the cutest little sweethearts. Although Liz had her hands full, she was happy to be off bed rest.

Dannie's other brother, Jeff, lived in the second-floor apartment with his fiancée, Kat. They were still working out a wedding date. Kat was having trouble with her mother about where the wedding would be. Kat's parents lived in Long Island and wanted her and Jeff's wedding to be some elaborate function. So, her father could invite all his lawyer associates. Jeff's plan was to go to Vegas and get married to relieve the stress it was putting on Kat.

Dannie's future sister-in-law had moved from NYC, where she was Liz's agent, along with some other big-time clients, but she gave it all up. She wanted to start a wellness center for women. The idea was, in part, because Kat was date-raped when she was in high school. She wanted to help not only women that had been raped but women that struggled in other aspects in their lives. She planned to have physical fitness classes, daycare, after-school programs for single mothers, and all kinds of self-improvement classes. Dannie even agreed to help by teaching a class on building your own website for small business owners.

Now that both her brothers were married or on their way to being married. Her mother would focus on Dannie, and for some reason, she had picked Leo for her. She knew her mother well and how she could put her superpowers to work. Linda was sneaky and slowly wore you down until you believed you wanted what she wanted. Oh, she did it all in the name of love. She wanted all her children to be happy. If she got a few grandkids, she was good. But, her mother didn't know anything about her break up with Todd and why she came back home. And if she could help it, she would never know.

Dannie did the boss-employee relationship, and look how that worked out for her. That was one of the reasons she wouldn't get involved with Leo. She was his boss, technically. Besides, she was taking a break from all men, no matter how hot. Todd left her with a ton of issues about her body, her abilities, and the emotional head games he liked to play.

After she caught him cheating, she couldn't do anything right. She worked on the biggest accounts, and they were happy with her work, but not Todd. He complained about what colors she used for the graphics the clients wanted. He said it was her fault he cheated, even though she knew that was bull-shit, the things he said about her being fat. Maybe if she lost a few pounds, he wouldn't have looked somewhere else. She would be more attractive if she did something with her hair or dressed better.

Todd made working there unbearable, and when she realized, he was going to fire her so his new girlfriend could watch, she quit. Oh, she didn't just walk out, he had left the door open for the new girl to see, so Dannie took advantage of the lack of privacy and blasted him for everyone to see and hear. Dannie knew by doing so, she wouldn't work for another big web designing company again, but somehow, it felt worth it at the time. She walked out of there with her head held high, and she made it to the parking lot before she started to cry.

It had almost been a year since she quit her job, and now she would rebuild the surf shop website. Ben had given her the go-ahead once he returned to work full time after the twins were born. Jeff was still working on the Shafford Boards product line and doing a great job. The surf shop was selling more Shafford products than they required in their contract. Once she got the website up and running, they would look for a warehouse to stock the products for the online sales. The website would be all her baby, and she was ready to sink her teeth into it.

Once Dannie was in her apartment, the first thing she did was get out of that stupid dress. Why she wore it, she didn't know, but her pajamas were calling her name. The thought of going down to the shop briefly passed through her mind. But she talked herself out of it. Dannie planned to go to head to bed. She had a new book and wanted to get lost in it. If men were off-limits in real life, she could at least fall in love in a made-up world.

Dannie snuggled under her covers and opened her book. She started reading, and the opening line was about how the heroine couldn't pick the right guy. No matter how Dannie tried, the men always turned out to be the wrong ones. So, she decided not to seek out a guy anymore. He would have to come to her, and then she'd consider if he was right.

The heroine walked down the sidewalk in the park. She must have disturbed a nest of bees because suddenly, there they were, swarming around her head. She started flailing her arms as she ran, screaming to get away from them, and ran right into a man. As he caught her, they both landed hard on the ground with her on top of him. The man had to think she was crazy.

Dannie thought if her life was only like that, she had the part of picking the wrong guy down pat. But finding the perfect guy, not so much. Her dating report card would have a big fat F on it. She closed the book and turned out the light. Plumping up her pillow, she closed her eyes.

The image of Leo answering his door in only a pair of board shorts vividly invaded her mind. How her eyes sought every inch of his body. The dark tone of his skin gave the perfect shadow to show off his muscle definition. He was a big man. She'd give him that, dark and intense. The way his eyes were almost black, and how he could look right through her with them. God, then there was the hair on his broad chest that worked its way down his abs and then disappeared into his shorts that sat low on his hips.

"Argh, I'm thinking about him," she rolled over. "Think about something else, work. The shop is closed tomorrow, so you can get started on the site. Yes, Dannie, think about writing code." She relaxed again, only to have Leo creep back into her mind, and each time, she squashed the thought of him.

The next morning, Dannie had her coffee and got dressed in some sweats. Brushing her teeth and putting her hair up in her usual knot style. She was heading to her office. No one would be at the shop, so she figured she could get a lot done. To her surprise, she wasn't the only one thinking that. Jeff had Owen and Leo work, changing around the back-storage room, now that they had cleared it out after the big black-Friday sale they had. Owen had worked for the shop ever since he took Ben's surf clinic as a young teen. He was like her little brother. He was going to Community College and now working in the shop part-time around his classes. Ben was helping Owen by paying for his schooling, so Ben wanted that to come first.

When she passed Owen, he bumped her with his shoulder, "You here to help us?"

"Not a chance, dweeb," she shoved him back. He just smiled at her. She kept walking to her office but met Leo in the hallway. "Morning," she said as cheerful as she could pull off, walking right by him. She could feel him watching her go. At least something inside of her hoped he was. Once she closed her office door, she leaned against it, taking a few deep breaths. "Okay, now down to business," she went to her desk and started her computer.

For the next few hours, she had her head in her computer until someone knocked on her door. "Come in," she looked up when the door opened. Jeff walked in, "We're ordering some lunch from the deli. You want anything?"

"Lunch?" Dannie looked at the time on her screen, and sure enough, it was after one in the afternoon. "Wow, where did the time go? It feels like I just sat down." Jeff sat in the chair on the other side of her desk.

"Yeah, we been working hard, too. But a meal, we don't miss all too often. You want anything?"

"Yeah, get me a turkey salad, no chips or bread, and a water."

Jeff made a face of dislike, "Just a salad and water?"

"I think I just said that, didn't I?" Jeff got up and started out but turned back to her.

"You will get chips because not only does it come with it, but I'll eat them."

213

"Whatever," she said and went back to her computer once Jeff left her office. She noticed he didn't shut her door, so not only could she hear the guys talking, but she could see them as they walked by her door. She could get up and shut it but figured the food would be here soon enough.

Dannie was entranced by her work. She was biting the inside of her cheek. It was a habit she did when considering what she would do next.

Once the food had arrived, Leo was sent to deliver Dannie her lunch. Jeff had commented that it wasn't much of a lunch at all. Dannie was deep in thought, and he was watching her while she didn't know he was there. She was pressing her knuckle into her cheek as if she was biting it. Leo's mind went to biting her in other places, as if she sensed his mind going where it shouldn't. She looked up.

He held up the bag, "I have your lunch." As if that's why he was standing there.

"Thanks," she reached out her hand.

Leo walked up to the edge of her desk, and the way she looked up at him gave him the perfect advantage point to see the cleavage her large sagging shirt displayed. All too soon, he handed her the bag, and the view was gone. Before he could walk out, she spoke.

"About yesterday, I'm sorry for coming to your place uninvited, and it won't happen again. I don't want to give you the wrong idea. I was just a little shocked to see you in just board shorts when you opened your door."

"Nothing more than what you'd see out on the beach, Dannie."

"Right, anyway, I'm sorry."

"Don't be," he walked out. He didn't want Dannie to apologize for checking him out or regretting going to his place. He hated that.

214

When he opened his door to her, he was just as shocked to see her standing there. The red dress she was wore, to the low heels, she had on. He had never seen her dressed up. She was always dressed like she was today, her clothes too big and baggie. Her hair was tied up and no make-up on, not that she wasn't beautiful. She just made sure to go under the sexier-then-hell radar. As if that was possible.

He wondered why she didn't want to be noticed? Why would she not want a man to see her for who she was? Because what he could see, he liked. *Hold back, Dude, she just apologized for coming to your place, and she is your boss. It might be time to find a new job.* Leo went back to work thinking about Dannie and the nice view he had earlier.

Dannie ate her lunch and was still hungry, but she needed to cut back. Today was the day she decided she would lose weight, and with it being the official day after the holidays, it was as good as any reason. It had nothing to do with Todd telling her she was fat because she knew she wasn't, but not far from it. She wanted to feel good about herself, and that was the only reason she wanted this.

Kat was starting up some yoga classes out on the beach after the first of the year. She was planning to do it for Liz and herself because Liz was trying to lose her baby weight. It was a way to get the word out about starting the wellness center for women. She had cards printed up and would hand them out to anyone who showed interest in taking her class. Kat had gotten certified to teach just before the holidays. She had been taking classes herself for years, and it was more of a technicality for her. Kat had a body Dannie would die for but worked extremely hard for that body. Kat was all lean muscle, and she watched what she ate, and Dannie knew she wouldn't have that kind of dedication. But, she did want to lose some weight, and if being a little hungry was what she had to do, then so be it.

Dannie heard her brother yelling that they were leaving, and he would lock up behind them. The shop became quiet, and that's when she went back to work. The website Dannie was building for the shop had many different levels, and one of the reasons she wanted it to be amazing. One was for the shop itself and how she wanted this to be her stamp on it. It would show Todd she still had what it took to work and put out an astonishing site. Something he no longer could take credit for because he loved to do that. He often took the recognition for her work from the clients because she never spoke directly with them. But she was told by others who were at meetings that he did it all the time, saying he directed his team.

"What a bunch of bullshit. I wonder if the new girl has caught on yet?" The biggest thing Todd did was come up from behind her, pretending to check her work, looking over her shoulder as he looked down her shirt. He would put his hands on each of her shoulders, squeezing them together as he put his weight on her to ensure a better view. At first, she liked the attention he showed her, and when he asked her to work late, she was thrilled. One thing led to another, and then they were a couple, not that she could share it with anyone from work. That should have been her first clue that something wasn't right. Oh, he told her some crap about people would claim favoritism if they knew they were sleeping together.

Now she was working for only herself and the shop. When her stomach growled loudly, she realized how late it was. She saved her work and shut her computer. This was half the problem. She sat at a desk all day. She hadn't even gotten up to use the restroom, and now she was going to eat again.

~ ~ ~ ~ ~ ~

After talking to Dannie earlier, Leo convinced himself to move on and not think about what he couldn't have. So, he asked the cashier out from the store where he always bought his food for some pizza, and she said she was free that night. He picked her up, and the more time he spent with her, the more he knew she wasn't his type. She went on and on about her cat and the funny things it did. Leo was bored out of his mind. He was looking out the window when he saw her get out of her van. His eyes tracked her movements as she opened the door and went to the counter.

Dannie ordered and then turned. He knew the second she spotted him on a date. She looked away quickly and didn't glance his way again. He hated the fact that he had asked this person out before, but now he was kicking himself. Dannie stood where they couldn't see each other, waiting for her food, but he knew she was there. Right in the middle of his date's story about how her cat got caught on something or another. Leo excused himself and got up, walking straight to where Dannie stood.

"I need your help. I'm on a date from hell. If she tells one more story about her cat, I'm going to kill myself." Dannie's brows pinched together, and she appeared to be confused by his statement as she looked up at him. The thought of kissing that confusion off her face passed through his mind.

"Sorry, but that's your problem. I'm getting my dinner and going home to eat and read my book. You're on your own." She turned to the counter guy and asked, "My food ready yet?"

"Yep, it's right here," he bagged it up for her, "Here you go, Dannie. Is there anything else I can get you?"

"That's it, Joe, thanks." When she went to step around Leo, he reached out to take her arm to stop her. She looked at his hand on her.

"Wait, Dannie, help me, please."

"Fine, but I'll do it on one condition."

"Anything," with the way he said it, made her brows go up.

"You have to stay here and let me speak to her."

He watched Dannie go over to his date, she spoke for a minute, and the woman got up and walked out. Dannie looked back at him and did the same. Leo paid the bill, wondering what Dannie had said to her to make her leave. He caught up with Dannie getting in her van.

"What did you say to her to get rid of her? You weren't mean to her? I wanted her to go away but not hurt her feelings."

"Quit fussing, you wanted her gone, and she is." Dannie went to close her door, but he stepped in to stop her.

"Dannie, what did you say to her," suddenly, he had a bad feeling about this.

"I told her you were gay and still trying to be straight. She could save herself a lot of trouble if she just walked away now. If you don't mind, step back so I can get to my own date, he doesn't like waiting."

Leo questioned, "You have a date?" He could hear his own shock, because she had said she wasn't dating anyone. She was taking a break.

"I already told you, now step back," she put her hand on his chest to give him a nudge. He didn't budge, and her hand stayed on his chest. She could feel the hard muscles under her hand tighten as if he was puffing up his chest.

"You told me you were taking a break from dating."

"I said, I don't date employees either, but my date is with a book. So, if you don't mind, I would like to get back to it." She shoved him harder, and this time he moved. Once her door was closed, Dannie wanted to bang her head on the steering wheel, but he was still standing there watching her. The way he got possessive when he thought she was going out with someone else and then she had to tell him, she had a date with a book, how lame.

Leo stood there watching Dannie's van disappear around the corner. He let out a frustrating breath. That was two women that couldn't get away from him fast enough. It didn't matter that he didn't want one, and the other he couldn't have. He was batting one hundred percent tonight. He shook his head with the thought of his behavior when he thought Dannie was going out with some other dude. She wanted him to back up, and he didn't. He needed to listen to her words and stop reading what he wanted to see in her eyes. He put his hand over the spot on his chest where hers had just been. Damn, he needed to get a grip on his attraction for her.

Leo went for his own car. He would be heading home alone again tonight. Not that he wanted to have sex with his date because he knew who he would be thinking about. Not all female companionship was the same, as far as Leo was concerned. Like if he could convince Dannie to spend the night with him. He knew that would be better sex than anything he had to compare it to because of how he felt when she was close to him. When she touched him tonight, he wanted to crowd her with his big body. Dannie had something, he couldn't quite figure out what it was, but he was drawn to it. She said no with her words, but her body and eyes said yes, please.

Leo went back to his place and changed into the board shorts he had on the other night. His place was too small, and the walls closed in on him, so he went out to the hammock he had stretched between two trees. Putting his hands behind his head, he closed his eyes. The vision of Dannie's cleavage on display was before him. The way they curved away from one another, there was just enough room to slide his dick between her boobs. Hot damn, that thought had him hard and wanting her more than anything or anyone. He let the fantasy play out in his mind. Every time he moved between her tits, she put her mouth on him, sucking the head of his cock until it popped from her delicious lips. That was all it took.

Find

Breaking Waves of Love

Book 3 of the Jacob's series

on Amazon or order a signed copy on

TrishCollinsAuthor.net

Made in the USA
Columbia, SC
07 February 2025

52584871R00124